# CITY OF
# SECRETS

Center Point
Large Print

Also by Stewart O'Nan and available from
Center Point Large Print:

*The Odds*
*West of Sunset*

**This Large Print Book carries the
Seal of Approval of N.A.V.H.**

# CITY OF SECRETS

# Stewart O'Nan

CENTER POINT LARGE PRINT
THORNDIKE, MAINE

This Center Point Large Print edition is published
in the year 2016 by arrangement with Viking,
an imprint of Penguin Publishing Group,
a division of Penguin Random House LLC.

The text of this Large Print edition is unabridged.
In other aspects, this book may vary
from the original edition.
Printed in the United States of America
on permanent paper.
Set in 16-point Times New Roman type.

ISBN: 978-1-62899-990-7


Library of Congress Cataloging-in-Publication Data

Names: O'Nan, Stewart, 1961– author.
Title: City of secrets / Stewart O'Nan.
Description: Center Point Large Print edition. | Thorndike, Maine :
Center Point Large Print, 2016. | ©2016
Identifiers: LCCN 2016010178 | ISBN 9781628999907
    (hardcover : alk. paper)
Subjects: LCSH: Israel—History—1948-1967—Fiction. | Large type
books. | GSAFD: Suspense fiction.
Classification: LCC PS3565.N316 C58 2016 | DDC 813/.54—dc23
LC record available at http://lccn.loc.gov/2016010178

Once again
to
Trudy

The angel of forgetfulness
is a blessed creature.

—*Menachem Begin*

# CITY OF
# SECRETS

# – 1 –

When the war came Brand was lucky, spared death because he was young and could fix an engine, unlike his wife Katya and his mother and father and baby sister Giggi, unlike his grandparents and aunts and uncles and cousins. A Latvian and a Jew, he was interned first by the Russians, then the Germans, then the Russians again. By chance, he lived. While he was tempted almost daily (really, nightly), he wasn't enough of a fatalist to return the gift. The winter after the war, with no home to go back to and no graves to venerate, he signed on a Maltese freighter and landed in Jerusalem, realizing his mother's life-long dream. In their dining room in Riga hung a bad lithograph of the walled city like a fortress out of *Beau Geste*, its stone golden in the numinous desert light. At the end of the seder, his Grandfather Udelson raised his glass to it. "Next year in Jerusalem." For Brand it was next year, without the sweetness.

Like so many refugees, he drove a taxi, provided, like his papers, by the underground. His new name was Jossi. His job was to listen— again, lucky, since as a prisoner he had years of experience. With his fair hair and grade school Hebrew, he could be trusted. The British soldiers, the blissful pilgrims, the gawking tourists all wanted to talk. They spoke to him as if he were slow, leaning in close behind his ear, shaping each syllable.

Where was he from? What did he think of the trials? How did he like living in Jerusalem?

"I like it," the man he was pretending to be said, instead of "It's better than the camps," or "I like living," or, honestly, "I don't know."

The city was a puzzle box built of symbols, a confusion of old and new, armored cars and donkeys in the streets, Bedouins and bankers. The Turks and Haredim, the showy Greek and Russian processions—everyone seemed to be in costume, reenacting the miraculous past. The very stones were secondhand, scavenged and fit back into place haphazardly, their Roman inscriptions inverted. It was the rainy season, and the walls were gray instead of golden, the souks teeming with rats. An east wind thrashed the poplars and olive trees, stirring up trash in cul-de-sacs, rattling windows. He'd lost too much weight during the war and couldn't get warm. When he ran out of kerosene, his contact Asher brought him a jerry can liberated from their masters. Nightly the streetlights flickered and the power went out. His flop off the station road overlooked the Armenian cemetery where

the whores took the soldiers after the bars ，
their electric torches weaving between
crypts. The rain fell on the domes and bell
towers and minarets, filling the ancient cisterns
beneath the Old City, fell on Mount Scopus
and the Mount of Olives and the desert beyond,
thunder cracking over the Dead Sea. The
dankness reminded Brand of his grandmother's
root cellar. As a boy he was afraid the door at
the top of the rough stairs would swing closed
of its own weight, the latch catching, leaving him
in darkness. Now he imagined her hiding there,
dirty-cheeked, surviving on jarred beets and
horseradish, but of course she couldn't be. The
house, the town, the entire country was gone.

Sometimes in the night when his dreams and
the lightning wouldn't let him sleep, he dressed
and went down to his taxi, an old black Peugeot
he kept buffed to a mirror-like shine, and drove
through the Zion Gate checkpoint into the Old
City, as if he were going to pick up a fare, to see
the widow. Her name was Eva, but when Asher
had recommended her, he called her The Widow
as if it were a code name, and though Brand was
a widower himself, he couldn't get it out of his
head. She would always be another's, that dead
love private, untouchable.

How, after everything, was he still proud?
There were worse things than second best.

Eva, his new Juliet, his new Eve. From Vilna,

the Jerusalem of the North, with an urbane scorn for backward Latvia. She was older than Brand by more than a decade, her eyes baggy, her jet hair threaded with gray. Before the war she'd been an actress known for her Nora and Lady Macbeth. She wished she had her clippings to show him. In the right light he could see she'd been striking once, the dark hair and sky-blue eyes, high cheekbones and generous lips, but at the corner of her mouth a deep scar had healed badly, the nerve severed so that one side drooped in an exaggerated frown, like the mask of tragedy. Like Brand, she hated the Russians and Germans equally, absolutely. She was a joke among their cell, a ruined woman, useful for one thing. When she drank, she railed against the world, calling all men pigs.

"Not you," she said. "You're like me."

How? he wanted to ask, but was afraid of the answer.

When she cried after lovemaking or while they ate breakfast at her small table, he knew it was for her husband, whose name she wouldn't say. Brand had no money, and they'd come to a loose arrangement he soon regretted. He was forbidden to mention the word love, would be banished at the first hint of romance. She was not his, merely a comrade. She taught him Hebrew and English a phrase at a time, correcting his fledgling attempts with her perfect articulation, as if training him for the stage. In return, he chauffeured her to her assignations, waiting discreetly across the street, smoking and reading the paper, trying not to think of Katya, whose memory had sustained him in the camps and through the long, starry watches at sea. After Katya, whatever happened to him was nothing. The world was not the world.

Tonight the Zion Gate was jammed, traffic backed up along the wall, the rain falling in long needles through a red fog of exhaust. The line was stopped. In the stark wash of floodlights shining down from the sandbagged ramparts, soldiers were going from car to car with dogs, opening doors, pulling people out. The police hadn't called curfew in weeks. There must have been an action, though the radio said nothing. He tried the underground station at the far end of the dial and got a blast of static.

Ahead, a soldier with a tommy gun was frisking a gray-bearded Arab in full robes and headdress while a dog nosed about inside the car, a grave insult if the man were Moslem, dogs being unclean. It was quite possible the man was a Christian; many of them were. Brand, being a transplant, couldn't tell them apart. He was more concerned that the dog would muddy his seats, and wished he hadn't thrown away his paper. It was too late to turn around, and he shut off his engine to save gas.

His papers were false, as was the Peugeot's registration, the car itself stolen from Tel Aviv, repainted and fitted with a smuggler's false-bottomed trunk. If taken in for questioning, Brand had no defense. He'd be detained as an illegal and a thief, interrogated, then jailed or deported, but all the times he'd been stopped, all the checkpoints he'd braved, the police had never challenged him. While his documents—like his current life, he might say—were passable forgeries, his livery license, a metal badge attached to the front bumper, and much harder to come by, was real. And yet, having been arrested before—once, in Riga, sitting in his booth in his favorite coffee shop—he knew that as a Jew you were never safe.

The dog clambered out of the Arab's car, its tongue lolling. The soldier with the gun motioned for the man to open his trunk. For a moment Brand expected someone to be in it—an assassin, perhaps—expected that person to spring out with a pistol and sprint for the darkness, only to be cut down by gunfire. There was nothing, just a spare tire and a cardboard box the soldier turned over, dumping in the mud a knot of embroidered scarves popular with the tourists. As he prodded them with the muzzle, the Arab turned his head and spat. Before he could turn back, the soldier with the dog stepped up with a baton and clubbed

16

him across the face, knocking him to the ground.

The dog charged, snarling, fangs bared, and as the old man scrabbled backward in the dirt, for a second—was it Brand's imagination?—he looked directly at Brand, eyes beseeching, as if Brand might save him.

Sorry, Brand thought, biting his lip as if still deciding. You shouldn't have spit.

The Tommy hauled the dog off by its collar. A squad came running, yanked the old man to his feet and hustled him away, bleeding, his robes muddied, leaving behind the pile of scarves and a single sandal. The soldier with the gun pulled the car off the road and left it there with the trunk open.

Brand moved up, straddling the scarves, and lowered his window. The soldier with the dog paused at the front of his car and noted his badge number.

"Papers."

Brand handed them over. The dog was panting, white froth on its tongue. In the silver light its breath was a cloud. In the camps he'd seen a guard dog shake a toddler like a doll. He'd never trust one again.

"Where are you going?" Unlike Brand's, the Tommy's Hebrew was flawless. It was always a shock to think a Jew could be brutal, let alone his enemy.

"The Jewish Quarter."

"What for?"

"I've got a fare there."

"What address?"

There was no reason to lie. He did anyway. "Seventeen Beersheba Street."

The soldier handed back his papers. "Go ahead."

"Thanks," Brand said, then, when he was well past him, his window closed, used a new word Eva had taught him: "Wanker."

The berm was lined with deserted cars, their doors and trunks flung open, bags and clothing scattered about the ground like trash. The Arabs must have pulled something big, because when he finally reached the gate, the police were loading a dozen of them onto a sand-colored bus with wire mesh over the windows. At the end of the line, the old man shuffled after the others with his head bent.

Inside the wall, the Armenian Quarter was dark, the iron grates of the cafés along the Street of the Martyrs locked for the night. The radio told Brand nothing, which was typical. The Mandate didn't broadcast its losses, only the glorious magnanimity of the Empire. He'd read about it in the *Post* tomorrow, with the obligatory editorial condemning both the Arabs and the British, as if their own position had somehow improved.

Like the rain, the constant politicking tired Brand out, and now, as he turned into the Street of the Jews, there was nowhere to park. He circled the Hurva Synagogue, searching, all the while recalling the old man's face. What was Brand supposed to do? His father had likely cried out the same way, and his mother. No one had saved them. On a snowy day, while Brand was tending the balky presses of a commandeered stamping plant, the Germans marched the Jews of Riga into Crow Forest and shot them. Not en masse but one by one, making each new victim lie facedown, naked, between the legs of the last, before delivering a single bullet behind the ear, the method designed not merely to break their spirit but to save space. He stopped himself from seeing Katya in the pit by squeezing the steering wheel as if he might crush it till his knuckles hurt, and cursed the old man and the soldier for making him remember. It was late and he was cold. All he wanted was to lie in Eva's warm bed and sleep.

A block in, the streets ended. The Quarter, like most of the Old City, was cloistered, a warren of stone. He found a spot by what was supposed to be a Roman bathhouse, ducked into the nearest lane and wormed his way back through the maze of cobbled alleys and wet steps, treacherous in the dark. The only sound was the rushing of downspouts, precious runoff sluicing along the gutters, dropping through the grates to the hidden cisterns below. Some nights, navigating

19

the shadowy labyrinth with its vaulted galleries and courtyards and bazaars, Brand felt as if he'd traveled back in time. Others, coming to her half drunk and wildly grateful to be alive, guarding the happy secret of his myopic, impossible love, he saw himself caught up in an exotic adventure. He knew they were both illusions, knew precisely why he needed them. He was no hero, no Romeo, just a fool, untouched as yet by the Angel of Forgetfulness. Now, as he walked the long arcade of the market with its shuttered stalls and through the arched gate behind Eva's boardinghouse, the lamp in her window that signaled she was busy confirmed his true station in the world.

He would wait. It was too late for pride. He'd done it before, in worse weather. In his flat there was nothing but the dregs of a bottle of arak, and tomorrow he had to get up and drive.

Farther down, there was a dry niche beneath the awning of a tinsmith's shop. From the shadows he could watch her door. He made for it, only to discover the flaring ember of a cigarette.

"Jossi," a voice he knew whispered, and the moon-like face of Lipschitz materialized from the darkness—his thick specs and piggy cheeks, a wet glint of teeth. "Asher said you'd come."

Brand liked Lipschitz well enough, but he'd be damned if he'd stand in line. "I'll come back."

"We tried calling your landlady."

"It's okay."

Lipschitz shook his head. "It's not that. We need your car." He pointed toward the door with his cigarette. "The password's 'Hezekiah.' "

Whatever the job was, after what happened at the checkpoint, Brand thought it couldn't be good. And it was slapdash, badly planned. Lipschitz, who could barely see, was their watchman.

When Brand knocked, the voice that asked for the password wasn't Asher's but that of a Frenchman. The man who opened the door was burly as a lumberjack, with bushy red eyebrows and a rusty beard and a stubby pistol he returned to his coat pocket. It was a serious breach of protocol. To protect the movement, you knew only the members of your cell. Neither mentioned it as the Frenchman led him up the stairs to the landing.

"Your taxi's here," the man announced, and closed the door behind Brand.

"Jossi," Asher called from the bedroom. "Get in here."

The lampshade had been tossed aside, and the covers. In the glare of the bare bulb, on the bed he'd hoped to share with her, Eva and Asher were holding down a shirtless man dark as an Arab. The white sheets were bright with blood— the room stank of it. The man moaned with his eyes closed, rolling his head on the pillow.

"Over here," Asher said, tipping his chin. Silver-haired and fit, he reminded Brand of his last ship's captain, a lover of port wine and chess. His hands were busy pressing a bloodstained towel into the man's stomach. "Hold this."

Asher stood, hunched so Brand could duck beneath him and take his place. The towel was wet and surprisingly warm. When Brand pressed it against the wound, the man grunted and tensed, his legs kicking.

"Keep the pressure on," Eva said. She held another towel to the man's shoulder while Asher went to the bureau and tore open a gauze dressing. He stripped white tape off a roll and snipped it with scissors.

Despite his dark skin, the man wore a gold Star of David on a chain and had a tattoo of a lion rampant on his biceps. Above his right eye branched a raised scar shaped like the letter yod. Probably a Sabra, born here. They were supposed to be the most ferocious, fighting for their homeland, not some bourgeois Ashkenazi pipe dream.

"Who is he?" Brand asked.

Neither of them said a word, and he realized his mistake.

Asher leaned across him, curling worms of tape hanging from his arm. He pushed Brand's hand aside to check the wound, the lipped skin holding a dark cup of blood. The hole could only be from a gunshot, Brand thought, a large caliber from the size of it. Asher packed it with gauze, making the man arch his back, covered it with another square and taped it in place. "Tonight he's your brother."

"Sorry."

"It's all right. Just think." Asher tapped his temple.

"Throw the towel in the washtub," Eva said. "And run some water on it."

The shoulder wasn't as bad, the shot having passed through cleanly, missing the bone. Asher and Eva bent over it, working like doctor and nurse, and Brand wondered how much practice they'd had, and how the man had ended up here.

Brand was relieved, thinking they were done.

"Don't just stand there," Eva said. "Help us roll him over."

When they did, Brand saw the exit wound.

Gauze wasn't enough. Asher plugged it as best as he could with a dishcloth, crisscrossing it with long strips of tape. The man had passed out. They sat him up to tug Asher's undershirt over his head. Already the blood was seeping through.

"Give me your sweater," Asher said.

Brand couldn't protest, but hesitated.

"I'll get you another," Asher said, and fit the man's arms in the sleeves. It was far too big for him. "Stand him up."

"Where are we going with him?"

"You're taking him to the Belgian hospice. A doctor will meet you there."

"My car's behind the synagogue."

"You'll have to get it."

Eva made to take his place, but Asher told her to go with Brand and called the Frenchman up from downstairs. Brand would bring the car around and she would run in and let the Frenchman know it was ready.

Outside, the darkness closed over them, a relief. In his niche, Lipschitz kept watch, squinting. They passed him as if he were invisible.

Brand didn't like any of it. He was nervous just being a courier. Without his sweater he was cold, and his fingers were tacky with blood. He wished he'd stayed in bed, and blamed the rain.

In the market Eva pulled his arm around her and they walked like lovers, a transparent disguise. "I tried to call."

"Lipschitz said."

"Don't be angry."

"Why should I be angry?"

"You did well," she said.

"I did?"

"You weren't afraid. You helped."

"Does this happen often?"

"It's not the first time, if that's what you mean."

He was quiet, and she reached up and kissed his cheek in apology. "It doesn't happen that often."

"I hope not."

"When it does, we have to be ready."

He understood, even as he flinched at the collective. Like everyone in their cell, without notice she was expected to turn her place into a safe house. He would do the same, and yet, remembering her and Asher working together and himself standing there with the towel like an idiot, he was jealous. He hadn't been brave, he'd been terrified, just as he'd been a coward at the chcckpoint with the old man. In the camps he'd learned to stand and watch. It had saved his life and made him useless. If he'd come here to change, he needed to do better.

Ahead, the alleys converged at a fountain.

"Where behind the synagogue?" Eva asked.

"By the baths."

She knew a quicker way, taking him through the flower market, the stones littered with stalks and wilted blossoms. A gated garden led to a park full of swishing cypresses whose busy shadows hid them. At its entrance they turned right through an arch, then left down a passage lined with dustbins and came out beside the baths. He expected an armored car on patrol, its spotlight sweeping the storefronts, but the street was empty.

As he stuck the key in the lock, beyond the city

walls the carillon of the YMCA chimed, striking two. He hadn't thought it was so late.

Eva sat in back like a passenger. There was no one until they made the turn onto her street, where a pair of headlights coming the other way flashed a challenge. The lights were too low to be an armored car, maybe a battle jeep left over from El Alamein.

It was just another cab trying to get through. Brand backed up and let him by, then pulled even with the mouth of her alley.

Eva leaned in close as if to pay and kissed his ear. "Be careful."

"You too."

Alone, he tried the radio. Nothing but static and, faintly, American dance music from Cairo—maracas and a snaky clarinet. *That old black magic has me in its spell, that old black magic that you weave so well.* Sometimes they danced to the phonograph in her sitting room, moving the table aside, and again he thought he should be asleep and warm, all of this a bad dream. He checked his mirrors as if someone might be sneaking up on him. Turning off his lights would only make him more conspicuous, so he sat with his wipers flipping, wasting gas. He watched the rain dimpling the puddles. He knew every step, every cobblestone between the street and her door, could make the walk blindfolded. They should have been back by now. Maybe the man had died. They'd still need to get rid of the body. But they could do it there, they didn't need his car for that.

A new song started, a tinkling piano and a boozy saxophone. *If you were mine, I could be a ruler of kings. And if you were mine, I could do such wonderful things.*

In the alley, shadows flew across the walls. From the darkness a figure emerged—Eva, with Asher and the Frenchman bulking behind, the man sagging between them like a drunk in Brand's sweater. From habit Brand hopped out and ran around to get the door for them.

"Get back in the car," Asher ordered, pointing.

In their rush to shove the man in, they knocked his head against the frame. He was dead weight, and they tried to prop him upright in the far corner. He toppled face-first against Brand.

"Lay him across the seat," Asher said, then to Brand, "Pull around to the back entrance. They'll be waiting for you."

"What's the word?"

"There's no word. They're expecting you. Go."

This time of night the Belgian hospice was a three-minute drive, tucked behind the Muristan in the Christian Quarter. There were no checkpoints to avoid. All Brand had to do was swing up through the Armenian Quarter. He turned off the radio as if the man were any passenger and focused on the road.

Ahead, past the shadowed colonnade of St. James Cathedral, loomed David's tower and the imposing block of the Citadel, backlit by the floodlights at the Jaffa Gate. He was a careful driver normally. Now he guided the Peugeot through the wet streets as if it were filled with explosives, slowing for every alley, rounding off each turn.

At David Street there was no white-gloved policeman on the little podium, no desert-colored jeep with a spotlight and machine gun mounted in back. Brand turned and eased by the darkened fish market. Beyond the broad piazza of the Muristan rose the Crusader bell tower of the Church of the Holy Sepulchre like a great black finger. Strange, Brand thought. Tomorrow he would take a dozen fares there and remember none of them.

Behind him the Sabra groaned, making Brand glance at the mirror. The man was sprawled across the backseat at such an angle that Brand couldn't see his face. The man moaned again as if trying to speak.

"Almost there," Brand said, and sped up.

The rear of the hospice was dark. As he pulled in, the doors swung open. Instead of the doctor Asher had promised, two men with bandanas over their faces like train robbers scurried down the steps.

Brand didn't get out. Without a word to him, the

men dragged his passenger out and shut the door, and Brand drove off, free again.

On his way back, as he slowed for David Street, an armored car crossed in front of him, headed for the Armenian Quarter.

"Baruch Hashem," Brand said, signaling, and went the other way.

Asher hadn't given him instructions on what to do after dropping the man off, but Brand had had enough for one night. He avoided the checkpoint by taking the Jaffa Gate, and then, safely beyond the walls, passing the Zion Gate, saw that traffic was still backed up.

At home, when he stepped out of the car, the ceiling light popped on. Across the backseat lay a wet swath of blood. He was lucky he hadn't been stopped. He closed the door and went and fetched a pot of water and spent a half hour and two of his best rags scrubbing the upholstery, telling himself it was a paltry sacrifice. It was a miracle, really, how much blood the body could lose and still go on. He knelt and dug in the seams, getting it under his fingernails, but some must have seeped through and been absorbed by the stuffing. Though none of his passengers complained, for weeks, whenever it rained, Brand could smell it.

# – 2 –

The man was Irgun. Overnight their handbills appeared, pasted on walls and lampposts around town, taking credit for a raid on the main police station, calling in the overbearing, didactic style of Marxist propaganda for open revolution. They were terrorists, inflicting violence directly on the British military, a tactic the Haganah, to which Brand and his cell belonged, violently opposed, since it turned world opinion against their cause. Killing British soldiers wouldn't make Britain change its immigration policy, and the crack-downs after the Irgun's raids made it harder for the Haganah to conduct operations. Only months ago they'd tried to wipe out the Irgun and the even more hard-line Stern Gang by collaborating with the police. Now Asher was giving the man Brand's sweater?

"Times change," Eva said. "We all want the same thing."

"All they want is our guns," Lipschitz said.

Asher saw combined operations as a way of gaining some control over the Irgun. No more freelancing. Every major action had to be approved beforehand.

"You can't keep a wolf on a leash," Fein said.

"You'd rather let it run wild?" Yellin asked.

Brand agreed with all of them. It was too late anyway.

The truce was followed by a lull, as if, having joined forces, the different factions couldn't agree on what to do next. It was the holiday season, and Brand was busy shuttling tourists to Bethlehem. His fellow drivers Pincus and Scheib let him in on a little scheme. A few of them chipped in to buy cases of film from a Rumanian wholesaler and sold rolls to their passengers at a markup. Brand, seen around the garage as a humorless greenhorn, acted scandalized but came up with his stake.

"I should feel bad," Pincus said, "corrupting an innocent like this."

"*Nu*, what?" Scheib said. "He's a grown man."

Smugly, like someone with a dire secret, Brand played along, letting them make fun of him. Privately he thought they couldn't mean it. That anyone who lived through the camps could be innocent had to be a joke.

And yet Pincus was right. While, like everyone, Brand had had dealings with the black market, he'd never been part of it. For the price, he shouldn't have been surprised the film was expired. He was a bad liar and a terrible profiteer, constantly aware that he was taking advantage of his fares. It was just film, not bullets or penicillin, but when they haggled with him, invariably, out of guilt or the need to be liked, he gave in. Only the Americans paid full price, a habit for which he was grateful, and soon he sold only to them.

"Will you take our picture?" they asked, standing by Absalom's Tomb or the Damascus Gate.

"Say cheese," Brand said.

Finally he had some money. The first thing he bought was a new sweater, the thickest he could find, a navy cable-knit made for skiers, decorated with snowflakes. The second was a radio so he could fall asleep to music.

For Eva he wanted to buy roses and jewelry and perfume. Her clients gave her gifts—nylons and Swiss chocolates were favorites—so why couldn't he? They would end up fighting, he knew, but, flush for the first time since before the war, he couldn't resist the grand gesture. After several visits to the tinker's bazaar, dithering over the hammered silver bracelets and rings laid out on silk squares, he settled on an amber pendant the Yemeni dealer claimed was good luck.

"Is for someone very special," the dealer asked.

"Yes," Brand confessed.

"She is already lucky."

Since it was expected, apologetically, in his

own inept way, Brand argued the man down a few shillings.

"Blessings be upon your house," the dealer said.

"And upon yours," Brand said, returning the bow.

He planned the evening like an action, checking the weather forecast against the calendar. He would surprise her with it on the full moon. To soften her up he bought champagne, the one gift she couldn't refuse, and the new Benny Goodman record. They would dance, and after, sprawled on the couch, laughing and half drunk, he would magically produce the pendant and offer it like a declaration. She would lift up her hair in back so he could fasten the clasp, and he would kiss her there. For days, as he drove the tourists up the Mount of Olives to watch the sunset, he pictured the moment when she would turn around and give him that crooked smile he'd come to love.

He could also see her throwing it at him, tearily beating his chest with her fists. Hadn't she specifically told him not to do this? Did he understand nothing?

So he was puzzled when, after the first half of his plan worked perfectly, instead of gratitude or histrionics, she accepted the pendant from him grimly, thanked him and set it aside.

"What's wrong?" he asked. "Don't you like it?"

"You shouldn't waste your money on me."

"I don't have anyone else to waste it on."

"That's the problem."

"Why?"

"Don't be stupid," she said. "You know why."

"I don't."

"Are you going to pay for my apartment?"

The question was unfair, sprung on him so bluntly. He resisted saying she could live with him. He didn't dare suggest he move in with her, and so had no answer.

"Don't be like that," she said, mimicking his pout. "Can't we just have a nice time?"

He wanted to take the pendant and leave, but where would he go? He agreed with her and drained his champagne.

"Come on," she said, taking his hand, "let's dance."

She spent the rest of the evening trying to cheer him up, letting him put the pendant on her and then wearing it to bed, and though he played along, Brand wouldn't be consoled. In the candlelight, her whispered urgings mocked him. It was all false, and long after she'd fallen asleep he lay beside her, contemplating her soft face and the monstrous scar. He would never know the woman she'd been, the bride and lively young wife. When had he become so senti-mental? She was an insult to Katya's memory. He was just lonely, marooned in a foreign city. It was no excuse, and he resolved never to fool himself again.

When he finally slept, he dreamed of the bleeding man, not in her bed but in his backseat, reaching for him as they drove through the Old City, trying to warn him of something, but when the man leaned in close, trying to speak, instead of words, out flew a gout of hot blood, drenching Brand's shirt, shocking him awake. He was naked and sweating. Beside him, Eva slept.

He wondered if the man had died. Asher never said, and there was no one he could ask.

In the morning as he was leaving, she thanked him for the pendant, as if to apologize for last night. From then on she wore it—to placate him, he thought—taking it off only for appointments, confusing him further. Instead of reassuring him, seeing her fish it from her purse and fasten it in the backseat as they curled down the drive of the Semiramis or the Mediterranean or the King David Hotel made him picture her naked in their bright, vacuumed rooms, and he gripped the steering wheel and fixed his eyes on the road.

At least he had money. He finished the arak and bought himself a bottle of Johnnie Walker. Now when he couldn't sleep, instead of his keys he reached for a glass. It was safer to stay home, with the extra patrols. In Cairo the bands played all night, the dial a warm orange glow in the dark. *Kiss me once, and kiss me twice, and kiss me once again.* Sick with pride, he stood at his cold window, looking out over the rocky graveyard and the black mass of the Church of the Dormition blotting out the Zion Gate and wondered if she was alone. Not once had she been to his room. In the small hours, the phone in the downstairs hall rang and rang. He listened for Mrs. Ohanesian to answer it, hoping it was her.

Days he still drove her. She didn't have to ask for him anymore. Greta the dispatcher knew. It was a joke around the garage. Brand the lady-killer. Brand the pimp.

Slovenly at home, Eva had a whole wardrobe of smart clothes for dates, picking through them with a critical eye as if choosing the right costume for a role. In public she wore an arsenal of hats with a netted veil that didn't quite hide her scar, a tease. In the backseat she opened her compact, lifted the veil and touched up her lipstick, drawing on a smile. The pendant rode her breastbone, the gold chain taut against her skin.

"How do I look?" she asked.

Expensive, Brand wanted to say. Cheap. Heartless.

"You look beautiful."

"You always say that."

"Because it's true."

"It can't always be true."

"Yes it can," Brand said.

"Stop, you're going to make me sick."

Brand's response, as always, was silence.

"Now you're not talking to me?"

With the influx of tourists, it was a busy season for her as well, her evenings booked solid. Christmas Eve he dropped her at the Eden Hotel and camped at the Café Alaska on the Jaffa Road, killing time drinking coffee and eating *Apfelstrudel* and reading about the war crimes trials in his old hometown paper from last week, his eye on the clock.

The Alaska was the province of a certain class of Mitteleuropean émigré now mostly extinct in its natural habitat. With its crystal chandeliers and polished brass samovars and marble-topped tables full of threadbare scholars playing chess and arguing politics, it belonged to Vienna or some other fashionable capital brimming with art and theater rather than gloomy Jerusalem, surrounded by nothing but rocks and Arabs. Like the kibbutzniks playing at being peasants, the Alaska's denizens clung to roles Brand, having survived the war, thought long obsolete. Yet there he was, reading last week's paper, fretting over the fate of a city that had murdered everyone he loved. He had his booth. The coffee was real, and the strudel wasn't bad either.

The Eden was just as fantastic, a dream from a bygone, triumphal era, out of scale, oblivious to human suffering. He was early to pick her up and sat at the curb with the motor off. There was a gala under way. One after another, gleaming limousines rolled up and disgorged couples in evening wear, the doorman salaaming as if they were royalty. British, most likely. Gentile, certainly, though he noticed some Indians and Africans and a pair of Arabs in Western dress. She was late now, and with every new arrival he grew more impatient.

What kept him from leaving? There was a whole queue of taxis down the street. She could just as easily take one of them instead of wasting his time. He made nothing chauffeuring her around, hated it.

As he pointlessly sharpened his argument, a grand Daimler from before the war pulled up, a car Brand associated with the German High Command, a particularly perverse affront here, though no one else seemed to notice. The doorman hurried to free its occupants. The blonde who ducked out and unfolded herself was slim and long-limbed as a ballerina, carrying a sequined clutch purse. The man behind her, silver-haired, in tails, complete with kid gloves as if they were attending the opera, was Asher.

Brand had never seen him in anything but khakis and a rough work shirt, his sleeves rolled to his elbows. He'd just assumed Asher was like himself, a tradesman of some kind, a mason or plumber, practical, good with his hands. Now, in the immaculate suit of a diplomat, there was something unnatural about him. Brand stared as if he were seeing a doppelgänger.

Without a glance in Brand's direction, Asher offered the woman his arm and ushered her inside.

Brand's first thought was that he'd stumbled into an operation. The Irgun were famous for their disguises, using Ben Yehuda Street tailors to copy British uniforms. The accursed car might be a message, rigged with TNT, Asher and the blonde agent packing Mausers. A Christmas party was the perfect setup for an assassination. Shots, then panic, an escape route through the kitchen, another car waiting out back.

He wondered if Eva knew and hadn't told him, if right now she was holding a deputy minister at gunpoint upstairs, the appointment a ruse.

He started the car. Any second he expected gunfire, the windows exploding in a spray of glass.

The Daimler tooled off and another limousine took its place, delivering another couple, older, the wife white-haired and stick-thin, the man rotund and red-faced, some sort of bureaucrat, though, Brand conceded with a scowl, they might be Irgun as well. For all he knew it could be the Irgun Christmas party.

After they'd disappeared, the doorman held the door open an extra moment and out came Eva. She turned to find him right where he said he'd be and smiled. Reliable Brand.

"Sorry," she said. "I ran into an old friend."

"Did you see Asher?"

She looked puzzled, as if she'd missed something.

"He just walked in."

"What's he doing here?"

"He was dressed for the big party. Any idea who it's for?"

"I can go back in and check."

"That's all right."

"Ask him." She pointed to the doorman.

Brand pulled forward and casually leaned across the seat. He made as if he were asking on her behalf.

The man poked his head in the window to address her. While he looked Arab, to Brand's surprise, like the soldier the other night, he spoke perfect Hebrew. "Every year the hospital has a party for the orphans. It's very nice."

"Thank you," Eva said, and then, when they were clear, "Hadassah Hospital."

"Maybe he works there."

"Or at the orphanage."

"He seemed to know what to do the other night."

40

"You think he's a doctor?"

"You know him better than I do."

"He's your contact," she said, "not mine."

"You've known him longer." Another surprise. Who was hers—Fein, maybe? Yellin? Lipschitz joined around the same time he did. Maybe it was someone from before, someone he'd never met. She didn't like to talk about her past, and he was afraid to guess at it. He didn't like to think about her present.

"I know he's married."

"Because of the ring?"

"Because of how he acts."

"You can tell that."

"That's easy."

"What else can you tell?"

"About him?"

"About anyone."

"I can tell when someone doesn't like women."

"Does he like women?"

"Yes."

"Do I like women?"

"Maybe too much."

"Maybe," he admitted.

"I told you," she said, fishing the pendant from her purse and sitting upright to fasten the clasp. "My grandmother had the sight."

What do you see for us? Brand was tempted to ask, but didn't want to know the future either.

"What do you know about Yellin?" he asked.

"What do I know about you?"

"Too much, actually."

"Don't worry about Yellin. If you have to worry about someone, worry about yourself."

He did. It was what he was trying to stop doing.

On the way back to the Old City they passed police headquarters, fortified by a double cordon of barbed wire. An armored car sat in front like the Sphinx, its main gun leveled at traffic. The façade bore the scars of the raid, the stone cratered and pocked from small arms, licks of soot crowning the blown-out windows. The Irgun had tossed satchel charges through the front doors and gone in firing. Brand had to remind himself that he was part of them now, and, in an unsettling way, they were part of him.

There was a long line at the Jaffa Gate, mobs of pilgrims streaming between the stopped cars and tour buses, flocking to the Christian Quarter for midnight services. The streets would be clogged with candlelight processions, and Brand swung down to the Zion Gate—only slightly better. As the pilgrims shuffled past, to keep their balance a few braced a hand against the Peugeot, gently rocking it. He'd have to wax it again.

"I used to love Christmas when I was little," Eva said.

"I always hated it," Brand said.

42

"Why?"

His reasons were so typical he just shrugged. "Why did you love it?"

"My grandmother on my father's side was Russian Orthodox. She made him get a tree for us so we could decorate it. She made little cakes with icing for my brother and me."

"Is this the one with the sight?"

"No, the other one. Christmas morning they'd come over and we'd eat her cakes and open presents. I remember one year I got ice skates and spent the whole afternoon showing off for everyone. When I took them off, my feet were covered with blisters. I loved those skates."

She'd never mentioned a brother before, and though she didn't say his name, he felt privileged, as if she were sharing a secret, giving him a glimpse of the girl she'd been. What could he reciprocate with?

"For my birthday once I got a submarine you put baking soda in so it zipped around underwater in the bathtub like a real one. When the ice was gone I took it down to the river with a friend of mine to see if it would work there."

"What happened?"

"It went down and never came up again. I guess I didn't use enough baking soda."

"I can just see you watching for it to come up."

"I really thought it would. It always had before."

"Poor Jossi. Life is disappointing."

"I don't think I was too upset about it."

"No?"

"There was always something else to do."

He told her about the railroad bridge he and his friends used to dive off, and she told him about her grandfather's apple orchard where she and her brother and her best friend Anya played hide-and-seek. He was picturing her in pigtails, climbing a tree, when ahead of them, all at once, as if an accident had been cleared, traffic moved. At the checkpoint the soldiers had given up searching every vehicle, and when they spotted his badge they waved him through.

Inside the gate, he turned for her neighborhood, leaving the sea of pilgrims behind. Except for a stray cat stalking along one wall, the Street of the Jews was deserted.

"Why don't you park?" she said. "There's a spot right there."

He offered the feeblest protest: "I don't know."

"You're not going to find a better one tonight."

It was unfair of her to paint his position in those terms, though no doubt true.

"You're probably right," he said, and pulled up. Before coming to Jerusalem, at best he'd been an average parallel parker. Now he could back into the tightest space with one hand. With enough practice, he thought, you could get used to anything.

In the alley, out of habit, he looked for the lamp in her window, but it was dark, the niche of the tinsmith empty.

She put the kettle on for tea, scrubbed the makeup from her face and changed into her flannel housecoat and slippers, an outfit at once dowdy and intimate. Though he could never be certain, he wanted to think he was seeing the real Eva, if not his, precisely, then, like the girl with the new ice skates, one unknown to the rest of the world. For all its confusion, love divined the truth. At bottom the heart was honest. Questioned long enough, it gave up its secrets, no matter how complicated or painful. Privately it was useless to deny them, a conclusion he came to later, when she was asleep and he was turning over the problem of Asher. His own problem was the opposite, Brand thought, but just as puzzling. With Eva, if fleetingly, he knew exactly who he was.

He woke at dawn to the call to prayer, a mournful wailing across the rooftops, inescapable. The muezzins were never on the same schedule, so that their keening seemed to echo from minaret to minaret, an insistent round. Eva didn't like mornings and kept her bedroom dark, her one window shuttered, a gap letting in a finger of light that drew a bright line across Brand's discarded pants. She slept on her back with her mouth slightly open, soughing, the chain of the pendant disappearing beneath the covers. He didn't want to leave her, but it would be a busy day on the Bethlehem Road. Each trip down was worth a pound, plus whatever film he sold. The sooner he got going, the more he'd make.

He kissed her cheek and she muttered and rolled away, burying her face.

"Merry Christmas," he said.

"You're waking me up."

"Aren't you going to make me some of your grandmother's cakes?"

"It's too early. You need powdered sugar."

"I have to go."

"No." Blindly she groped a hand behind her to keep him there.

"I'm sorry." He kissed it and folded it closed, patted the curve of her hip. "Go back to sleep."

"I'll make them tonight if you buy the sugar."

"It's a deal." He wasn't sure where he would find it, but all morning, surrounded by the white, alien desert, driving through the dust plumes of his fellow cabbies, he was happy, knowing she wasn't working that night.

Bethlehem was a madhouse. The grotto of the Church of the Nativity was a smoky hole where pilgrims from around the world stood in line to kneel and kiss the ground where Jesus was supposed to have been born, the spot marked with an ornate silver star. Only in Rome had he seen believers weep so freely. Some were overcome, fainting dead away, their cameras clattering to the marble floor. Others had fits, shaking and breaking into tongues. As with the Haredim and the yeshiva boys in their sidecurls madly davening at the Western Wall, or the shirtless flagellants scourging themselves bloody along the Via Dolorosa, such base displays embarrassed Brand. He'd never been seized by the spirit. As a child, to please his mother, he'd dutifully gone to shul and studied Torah with the other boys. His family was modern, like their neighbors, their congregation guided by a worldly minyan of lawyers and merchants and insurance agents. Even then Brand had been skeptical, his faith considered and intellectual, based on history and genealogy rather than any deep emotion. After his bar mitzvah he still celebrated the holidays with his family, but, like his father, an accountant and an eminently reasonable man, he no longer kept the Sabbath, and during the war stopped believing altogether. Now he found that kind of hysterical adoration not merely distasteful but baffling. As much as he'd tried to lose himself, he would never do it that way.

Only a handful of the pilgrims were ecstatic. Most were simple tourists, there to document their trip to the Holy Land for the folks back home and disappointed at the wax museum shabbiness of it all. He'd quickly picked up the tidbits they wanted to hear, pointing out the altar of the Magi and the manger with its swaddled doll of a Messiah, relating the story of the original crib, now silver-plated and preserved in St. Mary's basilica like a priceless family heirloom. He encouraged them to take pictures—safer and more personal than the postcards the pickpockets hawked outside—leading them up the tower of the Greek monastery with its distant view of the Dead Sea and stopping on the drive back so they could pose in front of the grotto where, that night so long ago, shepherds kept watch over their flocks. Sometimes, at the very end of the tour, saying goodbye, they asked Brand if they could take a picture with him. They shook his hand and tipped him, said they'd recommend him to their friends, and if that never happened, Brand appreciated the senti-ment. He thanked them and wished them a pleasant stay in Eretz Israel, never once complaining about the peanut shells and sticky drips of lemonade they left in his backseat.

Christmas was an easy day to make money. All told, Brand pocketed close to twenty pounds and made it back to the garage before five—plenty of time to find her sugar, he thought.

He expected the stores on King George Avenue to be closed, being British, but was surprised to find the Jewish strip along Princess

Mary shuttered as well. The owners of the Lebanese grocery in Mamilla Road had taken advantage of the holiday, and the Turkish bakery next to the French consulate. Who knew there were so many Gentiles in the city?

He thought he might find it at the spice market, and went from stall to stall, hounded by a pack of urchins grabbing at his pockets, demanding baksheesh. He reached the end of the arcade where the coffee souk started, the aroma from the steaming samovars distracting him, when, with the shock of the obvious, he thought: the Alaska.

They were open, and had some. Would they sell it to him? He didn't know how much she needed, and erred on the side of caution, asking for a whole pound. The price seemed high, but Brand gratefully handed the money over to Willi the manager.

"Merry Christmas," Brand told everyone as he was leaving, happy as Scrooge the morning after.

On his way to her place, with the sack on the passenger seat, he felt pleased with himself, like a husband hieing home from work with both a paycheck and the missing ingredient for dinner. It was dusk and pilgrims were swarming the Zion Gate, the floodlights adding an operatic touch, as if they were onstage for a crowd scene. There was no police bus, just the armored cars and the same Tommies with dogs. Brand pictured the soldier dumping the old man's scarves in the mud and thought of putting the sugar in the glove compart-ment but feared it would look suspicious. As the line moved up, he got his papers ready, and then, when it was his turn, the soldier with the perfect Hebrew wrote down his badge number and waved him through.

"Merry Christmas," Brand said. "Tosser."

In the Quarter he grabbed the first spot he saw and headed back through the web of alleys behind the Hurva. Her window was dark, and rather than celebrate the fact, irrationally he imagined she wasn't there—that she'd called another cab to take her to a last-minute assignation with a UN official the Jewish Agency hoped to blackmail. Climbing her stairs with the sack, he was pre-pared to knock on her door and stand there like the fool he promised he wouldn't be anymore, and then, as he reached the landing, as if walking into a bakery, he was greeted by the sweet, yeasty smell of fried dough.

Inside, the air was warm and cloying with cooking oil. He expected her to be happy about the sugar, but she didn't move to take it from him. She seemed cross, as if he'd done some-thing wrong. As if she'd reconsidered.

"Did you talk to Asher?" she asked.

When would he have talked to him? "No."

"Did you talk to anyone today?"

"I was working. What happened?"

"Asher's called a meeting for tomorrow."

There was no need to ask what it meant, and he set the sugar down on the table. "When?"

Noon, when they could use the excuse of the lunch hour.

"Where?"

"He'll let us know in the morning."

The endless precautions, at once frustrating and necessary. Brand thought the location could either be a clue to who Asher was or a feint. As with the Talmud, everything had meaning. Nothing was done by chance. The hard part was interpreting it correctly, a skill Brand knew he lacked.

She made the icing and decorated the little cakes, but the news left the two of them tentative and subdued, as if it might be their last night together. In bed, with the paraffin lamp just a jewel-like blue flame on her night table tinting her skin, he had to quash the urge to make promises.

"We should go to sleep," she said.

"We should."

"My mother used to say morning will be here soon enough."

"She's right," Brand said, and though it took hours, ultimately she was.

The meeting was out in the western suburbs, at a borrowed villa on a quiet street in Rehavia.

They gathered around the absent family's bare dinner table. On one wall hung the same dull reproduction of Millet's *The Gleaners* that decorated his grandmother's parlor. The entire cell was there, plus a special guest, the red-headed Frenchman, seated next to Asher, who introduced him as Victor. Asher didn't have to say Victor was a member of the Irgun, or what his rank was, merely gave him the floor.

In support of a wider action by combined forces, they were going to bomb an electrical substation in Ge'ula, a newer development northwest of the city. "Salvation," the name meant, a heavy burden for a suburb. The Frenchman made it sound easy. The substation was fenced but not fortified, and remote, tucked behind the Blumenfeld orphanage, away from the main roads.

Brand glanced at Eva, who nodded as if following along. It made sense that their first action would be in Asher's backyard. Brand suspected it was a diversion, and a minor one if the Irgun trusted them to do it. Maybe it was a test. The Irgun were known to make new recruits sign a loyalty oath in blood, pledging to fight to the death rather than be captured. Rumor had it they were issued cyanide pills, a contingency Brand would have appreciated during the war, but now seemed too late.

Were they still Haganah? He'd have to ask

Asher. And what about Victor's friend the Sabra?

Victor went on, laying out the operation as if ticking off a list. Case the target, set the charges, blow them on schedule and get out without being seen. They would be provided with materials—meaning, Brand supposed, explosives. The Frenchman seemed bored and impatient, letting his sentences trail off, as if working with them was beneath him. He would be their sole contact, no one else. He would speak only with Asher. If things went wrong, he would break off all communications, did they understand? They would be on their own.

Instead of questioning him, the rest of the cell listened, rapt, as if this was their destiny. There was no discussion, no doubts voiced aloud, or only later, when Fein and Yellin would have their usual kaffeeklatsch debate. For now they had their orders.

# – 3 –

Naturally he was tasked with transporting the bomb. The law was clear, and strict, trumped up and bent against them from the very beginning of the struggle. Possession of a weapon that might be used to kill agents of the Mandate carried a penalty of death by hanging. Though he'd fired it only once, during training, the long-barreled, antique Parabellum he'd swaddled in oilcloth and hidden in a looted crypt below his window qualified, as did participating in a conspiracy against the Crown, and the even vaguer associating with known terrorists. He'd been condemned to death before. It wasn't the worst thing in the world.

He was more afraid of blowing himself up, or others. He didn't know what compound they'd be using, how stable it would be, and as he cruised along the Street of the Prophets, he saw the sidewalks and bus stops of the commercial district lined with innocent victims. With every pothole he bumped over, he imagined the blast lifting the rear of the Peugeot off the ground and flipping it on its roof, jagged shrapnel felling pedestrians and smashing windows in a deadly radius.

"Don't worry," Asher said, "the stuff's harmless without a blasting cap," as if he had experience, and again Brand didn't know him. When the time came, Asher would show him how it all worked. It was a good skill to have, Asher said, as if they were talking about arc welding. Brand thought he'd be more comfortable with the idea if he'd fought in the war, a failing that ate at him daily. How many people had he killed by not fighting? How many in his barracks had he helped save? Not Koppelman, he reminded himself. That was the past. While he vowed he would never forget the dead, this was his war now.

As Victor promised, the substation was out of the way. Ge'ula was in the foothills and still under construction, framing crews busy throwing up cookie-cutter bungalows to claim the land. Asher sent Brand and Lipschitz to survey the area. The development sat on a treeless plateau, bald mountains looming over a grid of roughed-out streets. It was a bitter day, the blue Jerusalem sky a trick as they rocked past the skeletal shells with the heater blasting. When Brand spied the power lines festooned against a hillside, he stopped the car and they stepped out into the wind. Hammering echoed around them like gunfire. They walked the plots like prospective buyers, examining the painted stakes marking the properties. Beyond the last empty tract, the land dropped off sharply, giving on a wide ravine the lines swooped through. The slopes opposite were stitched with goat tracks. Brand couldn't see what they would eat.

"The land of milk and honey," he said.

"The goats like it well enough."

Lipschitz squinted into the light. Casually, in the neat hand of a draftsman—an engineer, or maybe an artist, Brand thought—he was sketching a map on a pad of graph paper, noting the position of each stanchion. The lines dipped south, following the contour of the land, and there, across a dry wadi, in the middle of open scrub, stood the substation, its fence topped with three strands of electrified wire. A pair of tire tracks ran cross-country toward the orphanage and its ring of outbuildings. A mile west the British maintained a base, the Schneller Barracks, including gas tanks and an ammo dump.

There were only the two approaches—down the ravine or across the flat. Brand didn't like either of them.

"Which way's easier, you think?"

"You mean which is worse."

"In the dark."

"We'll have the moon to go by."

"Half moon," Brand said. "Plus it might rain."

"If it rains, we get wet."

The plain could flood and Lipschitz would stay bone-dry. Only Brand and Asher were going this far. The rest would hang back and watch the roads, relaying coded information to the underground radio by phone. The Bukharan Quarter was just north of Ge'ula, Zikhron Moshe just south of the orphanage. Once they slipped into the backstreets, the British couldn't block all their escape routes. With a timer, they'd have a good head start.

"Those towers would be easy," Lipschitz said.

"You'd have to get the other side too. You get the station, you get both at once."

"So we're knocking out power to the orphanage."

"And the barracks. What else is south of here?"

"There's the hospital and the old-age home, that's all I can think of."

Only a local would know the old-age home, and Brand wondered if Lipschitz, with his black gabardine jacket and Polish accent, was from the mostly Ashkenazi Zikhron Moshe. He was younger than Brand, in his twenties, and pudgy, so he'd missed the camps. Unmarried. From his pallor and well-tended nails, he worked indoors. With his lank black hair, round face and shiny cheeks, he reminded Brand of Peter Lorre. Brand had known him only a month yet was trusting him with his life.

"Are there any pillboxes?" Brand asked, meaning the small, concrete-block kiosks the police had recently introduced to harass them.

"They're all to the north. It's got to be the barracks."

He hoped that wasn't their target. There were too many troops. "There must be something else."

"The reservoir's farther out."

"I don't think they'd hit the reservoir."

"You're probably right."

Barclays Bank, the central prison, the tax office. It was impossible not to speculate, and on the drive back, every police station and post office seemed a possibility. They weren't knocking out the power for nothing.

"We have enough blackouts as it is," Eva agreed. She'd heard from a girlfriend that the target might be RAF headquarters, across from the Damascus Gate.

Brand had dropped off fares there, and had once taken a carload of bubbly secretaries to the train station, one of whom had shared the front seat and given him an American cigarette.

He wasn't ruthless enough. He had to remember, this was the same RAF that refused to bomb the German rail lines to the camps, the same RAF that tracked the Aliyah Bet ships making for Haifa. He had to remember who his people were.

"I'm worried it might snow," Eva said.

"It doesn't snow here."

"It was cold enough today."

"I'm sure they'll take that into account," Brand said. "Actually it might help us."

"How?"

"They'll have fewer patrols out."

"I think you're being hopeful."

"I try," he said.

"Either that or you're an idiot."

"Also possible."

They drank and danced, the table shoved aside, and then in the middle of a song she lifted the needle from the record and took him by the hand. In her room, with the shutters closed and the lamp turned low, he could pretend the rest of the world didn't exist. Only this was real, and this, and this. It was a sweet lie, and so brief. In the morning she wept behind the bathroom door and his head hurt from the cognac. He understood her too well. What would Katya think of the man he'd become? The problem, he thought, was that he was still alive.

He wasn't weak enough to kill himself, but wasn't strong enough to stop wanting to. There was always the question of what to do with his old life, memory seething inside him like a disease. Not only his sorrow, but the guard stomping on Koppelman's face, the dog shaking the child, the wheels of the train slicing the idiot Gypsy boy in two—atrocities so commonplace that no one wanted to hear them. Everything he'd witnessed was his now, indelible yet unspeakable. His best chance was to forget, and so he kept on, letting the meaningless present distract him.

He was becoming a great liar. All day, as Jossi, he joked with his passengers, the Italian and French and Turks alike, while the buildings around them crumbled. Whenever he picked up a Tommy on leave, he was sure he was smiling too much, and felt the crazy urge to blurt out their plans. That would solve all his problems.

Maybe it would snow and they would call it off. Maybe the Peugeot would blow a gasket and they'd have to find someone else. And then, other times, he imagined dynamiting the gates and guard towers around the ghetto of Riga, setting everyone free. Was this so different?

Fein wished they knew the overall scope of the operation.

"I wish the filthy Arabs would go away," Yellin said, "but that's not going to happen either."

Brand trusted them because they were older and kvetched about everything like a long-married couple—like his uncles—but what better cover for informants? Had Asher been their contact, or whoever it was that had recruited Eva?

"I have no idea," Eva said, though, knowing her, he could see she was holding back.

"What?"

"You really shouldn't be asking me that."

"Who else am I going to ask?"

"I'm serious, Jossi. It's better not to know."

"I won't tell anyone, I promise."

"You don't know that," she said, as if he'd hurt

her, and he wondered what exactly had happened with her husband. He wanted to say he'd never leave her, but feared that would only make it worse.

The operation was everything now. They still had no date, but late Wednesday afternoon when he checked in with Greta from the call box at the Jaffa Gate, she gave him a pickup in Rehavia with a familiar address.

Asher was waiting on the porch with a black leather valise and a deep blue suit that might have belonged to a banker. In the backseat he kept the valise in his lap, his arms crossed over it as if it were filled with cash.

"Where are we going?"

"The high school," Asher said, as if Brand would know where it was. "Take a left after the Jewish Agency."

The quickest route was up King George. In the mirror, Asher watched the storefronts slide by, hooking back one cuff with a finger to check his watch like a stockbroker late for an appointment. Beside his perfect impersonation, Brand's own seemed crude, his bulky sweater a botched attempt at a costume—the greenhorn from Riga. He pictured the blonde from the limousine taking Asher's arm, and the smile she gave him. Was she his wife or was it just a disguise? He thought of Eva and himself. How much of their love was an act?

Like Rehavia, the high school was recent, and

bland, a concrete box in the unadorned style of the last decade. School was finished for the day; only a few cars dotted the lot. Asher had him park behind a Plymouth, hiding the Peugeot from the road, and they walked to the nearest set of doors. Asher knocked, and as they waited, Brand glanced at the valise and noted, just below the handle, a gold set of initials: NJW.

Nathan Joshua Weinberg.

Nahum Jacob Wertz.

If, in fact, it was his. Like the house, probably not.

The custodian who let them in seemed to know Asher, and again Brand marveled at the reach of the underground. The hallway was dark and quiet, muted daylight filtering in from the classrooms. At the end they pushed through a pair of fire doors guarding a stairwell. Brand expected they'd head down to the safety of the basement, but Asher led him up to the third floor, where he produced a single key from his jacket and entered a classroom. Beside the blackboard hung the periodic table. One wall was lined with glass cabinets ranked with flasks and beakers.

"What better place," Asher said, turning on the lights.

At the head of the room stood a long altar of a table with a sink at one end and several gas jets for demonstrations. Like a teacher, Asher hung up his suit jacket and rolled up his sleeves, opened the valise and began setting out its contents: a large dry cell battery, an alarm clock, a coil of black-coated wire, a coil of copper wire, a pair of tin snips, an awl, a screwdriver, some pliers, two jelly jars full of nuts and bolts, an oblong of a gray, clay-like compound wrapped like a fish in butcher paper, a tool like a conductor's ticket punch, and what appeared to be a stick of dynamite.

"Dynamite?" Brand guessed.

"And this is TNT. You're going to learn the difference between the two. Go ahead, you can touch it."

Brand gingerly picked up the stick and set it back down. It was surprisingly light, like a dry branch.

"Don't be afraid of it. You can drop it on the ground and set it on fire and it won't go off. Without a primary charge of some kind, it's harmless."

Brand, a fan of Hollywood Westerns in his youth, had assumed all you needed was a match.

*"This,"* Asher said, gently setting a silver tube the size of a fountain pen on the counter, "is what you need to be afraid of."

It was a blasting cap. One end of the tube was open to receive a fuse, the other packed with a small charge. Asher cut a short length of black-coated wire from the coil and picked up the ticket punch.

"You stick the fuse in all the way, then crimp the tube around it to keep it in place. The danger is, if you crimp it too close to the charge, it can go off. You just want to do the very end like this." He clamped the jaws of the crimper around the tube. "These things can be tricky. To be safe you want to hold it behind you and down, so if it goes off it gets your ass instead of your face."

He held it there a second as if he was going to squeeze it, and Brand braced for an explosion.

"We don't want to put the fuse in until we're ready to use it, so let's put this back. Just the end. In the old days, miners used to crimp them with their teeth, and every once in a while, boom. Look at the dynamite. See the hole there? That's for the blasting cap. Now this fuse I cut is way too short. Normally you want at least two feet. Safety fuse burns around thirty seconds a foot, sometimes a little longer or shorter depending on the weather. You don't want to go more than six feet, it's not practical. Anything longer than three minutes, you want to use an electrical charge, which is easier to use but harder to get. All of this stuff is hard to get, so we don't waste anything."

As Asher fixed wires to the dry cell and the alarm clock, Brand watched, frowning, trying to remember everything. Crimp the end, hold it behind you and below the waist, thirty seconds a foot, no more than six feet. Not knowing the difference between dynamite and TNT, he was sure he would blow his hand off on his first try.

"Where did you learn all this?"

"In the old days we had actual training. Now everything's rush-rush. Here, make yourself useful and wind this up."

He showed Brand how to rig a timer and how to booby-trap a door, how to poke a knot down the neck of a Molotov cocktail so the rag wouldn't come out when you threw it. The nuts and bolts were shrapnel for homemade grenades. Again and again they went back to the blasting cap and crimping the fuse, fitting it into the TNT, until Brand was convinced this was how they were doing the substation. Asher kept checking his watch, and after a last demonstration on pressure mines, began packing everything into the valise.

"Any questions?"

"So, what's the difference between dynamite and TNT?"

"Ah, you *were* listening. TNT is more stable, more powerful and works when it's wet. Which is why it's always preferable over dynamite, and why it costs more."

"Is that what we're using?"

"We don't know yet. It would be nice."

Asher pulled on his jacket and locked the door behind them. Teacher or doctor, businessman or electrician, he had a heartening confidence. His accent was Slavic, maybe Czech, yet he showed no sign of having been in the camps.

Now that Brand had him alone, he wanted to ask him what he'd done during the war. Instead, he thanked him for the lesson.

"It's good," Asher said. "Everyone should know these things."

Brand thought Asher was downplaying both his generosity and the singularity of the subject matter until Eva asked if they'd gone to the high school.

"Did he tell you about the miners?" She bit down on an imaginary blasting cap. "He loves to scare people with that old wives' tale."

Before this, Brand had taken his going along as Asher's backup as confirmation that he was second in command. Now he realized that—as always—it was because he had the car. Eva, Fein and Yellin, possibly even Lipschitz knew how to set off a bomb. Why was he always surprised to discover he was wrong? By now he thought he should be used to it.

As Eva had forecast, the snow came, falling overnight, softening the graves beneath his window, topping the city walls like frosting. The tourists were thrilled, snapping away at the domes and the olive groves, and all day he was busy. The Peugeot's wheels spun in the slush. It reminded him of Riga and his grandmother's warm kitchen, the tiled niche beside her oven where he drank hot cocoa after playing outside, the feeling returning to his cheeks. Back in his flat he kept his sweater on and turned up his Primus stove as high as it would go, nipping at his Johnnie Walker, and still he was freezing. Below, Mrs. Ohanesian picked at the *Moonlight Sonata*, trying the opening bars over and over, her budgerigar chittering like a critic, until, mercifully, she conceded defeat.

He thought the snow would be gone the next morning, but it lingered, further postponing the operation. The longer they waited, Brand reasoned, the more dangerous it would be, with so many people knowing at least a piece of the plan. He'd begun to hope it would be canceled altogether when, late that night as he was listening to Trieste under the covers, the phone rang downstairs and Mrs. Ohanesian hollered for him.

"The Edison Cinema," Asher said. "Eight o'clock tomorrow."

"That's fine, thanks," Brand said, because behind her door Mrs. Ohanesian would be listening. While he was let down, he wished he could pull on his jacket and go right now, if only so he didn't have to wait another day.

Standing there, he weighed calling Eva, though she had to know, and decided not to. If the British were listening, he didn't want to make it easier for them.

When he woke, it was snowing, the Dome of the Rock just a shadow behind the swirling curtain. Had no one checked the weather?

The schools were closed, and the souks, the city wisely staying inside. All day Brand sloshed through the empty streets, feeling eyes on him as he passed the armored cars guarding the central prison. The underground had more fighters than guns. The police training school, the various barracks. Any armory, he supposed. How many weapons would a pillbox have? Even they were fortified. In comparison, the substation was easy pickings.

As the day faded, the wind shifted. The snow turned to freezing rain, and the fares disappeared, the tourists retreating to their hotels. Greta had nothing for him and he sat in the queue at the Jaffa Gate, reading the *Post* and listening to the Voice of Fighting Zion, waiting for his shift to end. Sleet ticked against the roof, crystals melted on the hood. The hillside would be impossible in this. They'd have just the one way in and out, cross-country. If they got stuck, they'd have to leave the car. Absurdly, he was worried about it as if it were his.

Back at the garage, Pincus asked him if he could take a look at his water pump, and though Brand just wanted to go home and get ready, he hefted his toolbox from his trunk. Pincus had a tiny Fiat that could fit down the tightest alley. During the war, parts were impossible to find, and the engine was a Frankenstein. Brand hung a utility light from the hood latch and poked his head in close over the hot block, weaving to stay out of his own shadow.

"Hoses look fine."

"I could tell you that," Pincus said, leaning in beside him.

"What's it been doing?"

"Nothing. You fixed it, boychik. Thank you. You can put your fancy tools away now."

Brand didn't understand. Pincus had to place his hand on the open lid and shoot him a double take before Brand recognized, among his pliers and wrenches, a black, snub-nosed pistol.

Pincus shut the lid. "I'm thinking maybe you can use it better than I can."

"Thank you," Brand said, more alarmed than grateful. Was there anyone in the city who didn't know? So often he felt like the last person in on the joke.

The gun was loaded, a death sentence if he were stopped. He left it in the trunk on the way home, though to the Mandate it didn't matter if it was locked up or in his hand.

The protocol for a direct action was empty pockets. He could bring the gun, but nothing that connected him to anyone. The movement had gone to some trouble to make sure the Peugeot was a dead end. Brand thought he wouldn't mind dying nameless. Katya had, and the rest of his family. He'd never liked Jossi anyway.

He took only his car keys, leaving his flat open. Most likely he'd be back, but as he descended the stairs for what might be the last time, his thoughts veered to the dramatic. Mrs. Ohanesian would take his radio and the wad of pounds in the cigar box. Below his window, the old Parabellum would rust shut in its grave.

The telephone in the hall made him want to call Eva. He should have had a last night with her, like a soldier shipping off to the front.

Stupid. He was only going to Ge'ula. With a tip, the fare was barely six shillings.

It was raining harder now, a spattering like frying fat surrounding him, muffling all other sounds. In the darkness he took the gun from the trunk and stuck it in his pocket, then, once the ceiling light went off, slipped it under his seat.

There was no one on the roads, and no crowd outside the Edison, only the marquee reflected in the wet pavement: *Spellbound*, with Gregory Peck and Ingrid Bergman. He was early, and circled the block, finding a spot across the street where he could see the doors. He wasn't sure why Asher chose so public a location, unless it was part of an alibi. What was wrong with the house in Rehavia? Again Brand felt helpless, as if the conspiracy were against him.

Right at eight, as the carillon of the YMCA struck the hour, Asher emerged from the cinema in a trench coat, as if he'd stepped out of the film. He raised a hand, and Brand swung the cab to the curb.

"Where to?"

"Turn on the radio. If they say 'Churchill' three times, it's off."

"Got it."

With the weather, the signal phased in and out, and Brand had to strain to hear the announcer, going on about the Ten Lost Tribes. Long before Lord Balfour, the Lord God promised His people both banks of the Jordan. Kol Hamagen was an arm of the Haganah, which was an arm of the Workers' Party, and while, after the camps, Brand considered himself apolitical, it bothered him when socialists based their arguments on scripture.

In the backseat Asher was unwrapping a package. "All they had was dynamite." He sounded unhappy about it, which made Brand unhappy.

"It's dry, right?"

"I'm sure it's fine, I'd just rather not take any chances."

It was too late for that, Brand thought, checking his mirror to see if they were being followed. No, they were the only ones foolish enough to be out in the monsoon.

As they splashed along Mea Shearim Street, skirting the Hasidic neighborhood, the street-lights showing them the road flickered and dimmed. The whole line flared once, twice, then died. Simultaneously, the radio cut out as if the transmitter had been hit, leaving only the shuttling of the wipers. Beyond his headlights, the night was as black as the middle of the ocean.

Brand's first thought was that the Irgun had knocked out the main power station, relieving them of their mission. More likely it was a blackout brought on by the storm, annoying but temporary. He focused on the road, expecting the lights to snap on at any second, revealing a hidden jeep or police car lying in wait, except as they burrowed deeper into the suburbs, there was nothing. He could get Amman and Damascus on the radio but not the government station, and he thought, with the hard pragmatism of a partisan, that it would be a good night to blow the antenna.

"You brought a torch?" Asher asked.

"I brought everything you told me to." Meaning the bolt cutters and tin snips and rubber gloves. They were ready for any contingency, though he no longer felt like doing it at all. On a night like tonight, he should be at Eva's, keeping warm.

A gust pushed the car and he pulled it back into the lane.

"How's the wind?" Asher asked.

"Bad."

They were into Zikhron Moshe now, cruising

past the skimpy business district, the unfinished streets of Ge'ula somewhere off to their right. In the hills beyond, the Arab villages were dark year-round, their houses lit by cooking fires and candles and the rare kerosene lamp, as in the last century. The wadis would be running high and muddy, the ravine flooded. Churchill, Churchill, Churchill, Brand wished, but they kept on. In back Asher flicked a lighter, the flash startling Brand like a shot.

"I think we'll be all right," Asher said.

The Zion Blumenfeld Orphanage was just past Zikhron Moshe, a sprawling farm complex dedicated to raising the displaced children of the war in a pastoral utopia. Here, packed into dormitories like laagers ringing a rustic stone temple, refugees from the bloody capitals of Warsaw and Prague and Vienna learned how to nurse calves and pluck chickens. Brand slowed well before the main entrance of the campus and turned down an unpaved road owned by the power company. The road ran along a fence line behind a row of barns. Trucks had dug deep ruts, leaving a hump in the middle Brand had to keep one wheel on so the Peugeot didn't get hung up. Its rear slipped in the mud, and they slid sideways, their headlights sweeping the sky. He tried to go slowly, but rocks still knocked against the undercarriage. He could imagine one cracking his oil pan, stranding them. They'd have to use the bomb on the car and walk home.

They left the protection of the barns and set out across open space. He imagined how they must look from the road, the only lights for miles. The patrols would have to know they didn't belong there. If it wasn't raining, he could have turned his lights off and navigated by the stars. Instead, he kept a wheel on the hump and aimed straight ahead.

"We should be seeing it in a minute," Asher said.

He was trying to be calm, Brand thought, talking just to talk. Where else would it be?

Once, in the harbor at Marseilles, a launch he was on lost its engine in heavy swells. It was June, and the sea was too cold to survive for more than a few minutes. Each time the launch dropped into a trough, it took on more water. The first mate had the cowling of the engine off, franti-cally yanking the cord. Brand could see the shore, maybe a kilometer away. In perfect weather, with a friendly current, he might swim for it, but that day he knew he'd never make it. After living through the camps, he was about to be killed by a fouled spark plug, and sitting there soaked and shivering, he reviewed his life and accepted his fate. The same strange peace overcame him now. He was glad he loved Eva, and he was proud to fight for Eretz Israel. If he should die tonight, he regretted nothing.

"There's a pylon," Asher said.

When Brand had cased the substation with Lipschitz, they'd been too far away to gauge the tower's real size. Close up, it rose like an oil derrick. At the top, giant insulators jutted from its frame like raised arms. The concrete pad at the base was several meters thick. A stick of dynamite would do nothing.

The substation was more approachable, the spindly array reminding him of Ge'ula's skeletal houses. He killed the lights and turned the car around, kept it running.

Now that they were here, they had to act fast. There was no talk. They knew what they had to do.

Only the wires around the top of the fence were electrified. While Brand hunched in the rain, chopping at the lock with the bolt cutters, Asher sat in the dry backseat, fitting the fuse into the blasting cap by the light of the torch. If he made a mistake now, Brand would hear it.

He was done first, and hopped back in the driver's seat.

Asher cracked the door an inch, thumbed the wheel of his lighter and set the flame to the fuse. It sizzled, and he pushed through the door into the rain.

Brand put the car in gear and waited with the door open. He wasn't sure if Asher had purposely left the torch on. The beam picked out the seams of the backseat, making him recall the Sabra.

Asher ducked through the door. "Go."

Brand drove.

"We should have at least three minutes." Asher was breathing hard from running. For some reason, Brand thought it was funny.

He tried to keep a wheel on the hump but they were going too fast. He swerved, and the stones clunked underneath them. It was quicker coming back, knowing where they were going. They rattled past the barns and made it to the main road with a minute to spare.

"Where are we going?"

"Back to the Edison."

They took the darkened side streets, sneaking down through Zikhron Moshe toward the bus station, keeping to the speed limit. With every passing block, they were safer, just a cabbie and his fare. Instead of relief, Brand was aware of the gun under his seat.

Even in the rain, the Egged station was busy, the buses idling in their spaces, the passengers lit like fish in an aquarium.

"Time," Asher said, holding up his watch, but so far away, with the power still out and the rain falling all around, it was impossible to tell if the bomb had gone off. Brand thought it was a cheat. After all their trouble, he wanted to hear it.

# – 4 –

They would never know what happened exactly. Supposedly the target had been CID headquarters, brimming with intelligence and weapons and possible hostages, but the operation had been called off, most likely because of the weather. The government station reported that several power facilities had been attacked. Perforce, the Haganah denied any involvement. Though he knew the substation would be under surveillance, Brand wanted to drive out to Ge'ula with a pair of field glasses and see the damage for himself, as if to prove they'd actually done it. The closest he came was taking a fare to the old-age home, glimpsing the tower—intact, as were the wires—as he passed the bare fields of the orphanage. In retrospect, the mission seemed both heroic and foolhardy, but mainly disorganized. Brand was no soldier, yet again and again over the following days, as he tooled around town, telling stories of King Herod and the City of David, he pictured himself and Asher bumping along the stony road beside the barns in the dark, recalling the night not with honest dread but pride and a belated excitement. Crazily, he wanted to do it again.

Like bank robbers after a haul, they laid low. No meetings or phone calls, not even a coded message through Greta. Pincus didn't ask for the gun back, so Brand hid it in the crypt with the Parabellum after the whores and Tommies had finished their business. In the morning he woke, no longer condemned. He was a cabbie from Latvia named Jossi. He drove and sold film, ate his falafel for lunch sitting in the queue outside the Damascus Gate. Did he know where the Convent of the Cross was?

"You bet," he said.

The Hall of the Last Supper?

"No sweat."

In Jaffa a truck bomb went off outside the town hall, killing fourteen Arabs. That night the British shot a teenager pasting up handbills. Brand thought Asher would call, but stayed disciplined, keeping radio silence.

It was still Christmas. First for the Orthodox, then two weeks later the Armenians. The Peugeot reeked of incense. Even Eva was sick of it. She was tired of paying for bad black market coffee and Cyprian brandy and having to get dressed after supper and go out into the cold and rain so some pig of a bureaucrat could slobber over her. The nights she worked, she was never sober. To steel herself, she drank before she went out, then afterward drank to forget. She never brought up her rent again, but often when she ranted against the unfairness of the world, Brand thought it was his fault.

He had some money, but nowhere near enough. She was too strong to be kept anyway. He had to be satisfied, their rare nights off, with buying her dinner and taking her to the movies. He wasn't sure if they were courting. She dressed as if she were meeting a date, coordinating the same outfit she'd worn at the Fast Hotel last Tuesday, the only difference was that now she rode up front with him. She chose the place, a gangster hangout off Queen Melisande's Way. At the Kilimanjaro Supper Club the hatcheck girls and waiters all knew her name as if she were famous, her notoriety a kind of celebrity. Invariably their table was in a dim corner behind a beaded curtain, away from the other couples. Women glared at her back as she passed, leaned in to whisper. "Aditti," they muttered under their breath, slang for a girl who slept with the British. She was so private that he forgot she was a public scandal. He wished she would spin on her heel and slap their faces, but she kept walking as if she didn't hear. Though he knew she'd only be angry with him, like a knight, he wanted to defend her honor. Would it matter to these women that she was doing it for them?

"They have no right," he said.

"Let's have a nice time," she said. "Drink your drink."

Even here her scar drew stares, as he imagined her beauty had when she was younger. Before the war, the men in the room would have envied him. Now he expected they took him for her pimp or her gigolo. His second drink gave him the courage to make a joke of it.

"What do you care?" she asked.

"Because I'm neither."

"That's right, you're pure."

He was ready to leave as soon as he finished eating. She insisted on coffee and dessert, lingering over a refill as the place gradually emptied. Once the other customers had left, the maître d' Edouard came by their table to pay his respects.

"Miss Eva." He bowed in the continental manner and kissed her hand. It wasn't merely that she was a regular. His deference was deep-seated, verging on adoration. Every time he chatted her up, Brand was convinced he knew Victor and Asher, their conversation rife with hidden meaning. He hardly said a word to Brand, only hello and goodbye, as if they had no business.

"Why don't you like him?" Eva asked.

"Because of the way he looks at you."

"He's French." She shrugged, innocent. "Edouard's an old friend. He was a friend when I didn't have friends."

New himself, Brand understood her perfectly,

and still he worried. Everyone they met seemed to know her better than he did.

In the Edison, safely hidden in the dark, he could relax. Like a moony schoolboy, he held her hand, stole glances at her, rapt. She seemed happiest in the cinema, pointing out background details and the director's camera tricks, gripping his arm at moments of suspense. She loved Ingrid Bergman, her great soft face filling the screen.

"No one pouts like Bergman," she said, as if they were colleagues.

Bergman, Vivien Leigh, Gene Tierney—she became all the stars. On the way home she played her favorite lines, and he could imagine the actress she'd been. He wanted to kill whoever had ruined her face.

In bed, as she slept, he imagined Katya hovering in a corner of the room, an angel watching over him. She knew him to be sentimental at heart, despite his Swedish cynicism, inherited, like his green eyes, from his father, a lover of sunsets and protector of the weak. What would she think of him now, and what could he say to her?

After he was released, he'd taken the train out through the leafy countryside to Crow Forest the same way they'd been marched in the snow, but the ground had been dug up by the Russians, the bodies carted away in dump trucks and tipped into secret graves with the German dead, a second desecration. He walked the turned earth, searching for a scrap of cloth, a button, the steel frames from a pair of eyeglasses, any clue as to what had happened there. It was May, and the first shoots of grass had sprung up, fringing the mounds with green. All around, weeds and thistles grew knee-high, thriving reminders of the relentless business of life. He stood in the clearing, looking at the trees on all sides reaching for the sun, the birds flitting from branch to branch, calling to one another, and knew he had to leave. He found a smooth egg of a stone, knelt and placed it in the soft grass. A week later he signed on the *Eastern Star*. From the stern he watched the steeples of Riga dwindle as the ship steamed up the Daugava for the open sea. If he had a home now, this was it.

He hadn't heard from Asher in weeks. Some mornings, waking early and driving the empty streets, Brand could believe this quiet routine was his life, everything else a mad dream. And then one afternoon, dropping off a couple of tight-lipped RAF colonels at the English Sports Club, he rolled up the drive to find the blonde from the Eden looking lithe in a riding ensemble, her hair pulled back in a neat chignon, climbing into the driver's seat of the Daimler as a valet held the door.

The club was south of the city, by the train station. The quickest route back was Julian's

Way through the German Colony, which now, after the war, was mainly British. He watched the Daimler glide down the drive and turn left as he expected while the colonels compared handfuls of change. The taller haltingly counted out three hundred mils into Brand's palm—a minimal tip.

"Cheers," Brand said, and sped off.

Julian's Way would take her up between the YMCA and the King David and into the main business district at the Jaffa Road. This time of day the only traffic was a stray patrol and a few cabs bringing passengers from the two o'clock train. The Daimler was hard to miss, and by the Montefiore Windmill he had it in sight. A long touring car the gray of sharkskin, polished, like his Peugeot, to a wet gleam, it made him think of Rommel and goose-stepping parades.

Brand was hoping she would lead him somewhere or to something he could connect to Asher. As they sped along, climbing the rise of Mount Zion, he stayed three cars back, not wanting to spook her. As if she'd spotted him, as the Y's Jesus Tower rose ahead of them to the left, with-out signaling she braked and turned right into the King David.

While the rest of the hotel was open to the public, the Mandate rented the entire south wing for its more sensitive offices. An obvious target, the Secretariat had a separate entrance ringed by barbed wire. A pair of armed Tommies waited at a guardhouse, checking every visitor. The last time he'd dropped off a fare there—a soft-spoken undersecretary of agriculture—they'd opened the man's suitcases as if he might be one of the Stern Gang. As Brand shot past and the Daimler rolled up the main drive, the blonde gave the soldiers a wave as if she were a regular.

"Someone's mistress," Eva guessed. "Or someone's wild daughter. Maybe both."

"Why would she be with Asher?"

"He's using her for access."

"Why her?"

"Apparently she can get in anywhere."

It made sense, yet the idea, being incomplete, unsettled Brand. Shipboard, the captain let the crew know where they were going, and what the seas would be like. There wasn't another crew hidden belowdecks with a destination of their own.

According to protocol, he couldn't ask Asher, just as he couldn't discuss the truck bomb in Jaffa with anyone.

After her third glass of brandy, Eva would talk. Like an interrogator, he listened for the littlest slip.

"You weren't here for the riots. They killed hundreds of us. They broke down doors and cut children's throats. It's like they went mad."

"These weren't the same Arabs," he said.

"We're not the same Jews. That's the point. We won't sit around and be killed anymore. That's what they have to understand. We'll fight."

"I think they understand that now."

"You have to remind them, otherwise they'll go back to their old ways."

Like him, Brand thought. The New Jew, they called the Sabras. The other night he'd felt like one. Now he wasn't sure. His own philosophy was closer to the Jewish Agency's—nonviolent resistance—though they directly supported the Haganah, who'd ditched their policy of self-restraint when they joined with the Irgun and the Stern Gang, this after calling them dissidents and terrorists and helping the British hunt them down. Brand didn't understand how they were all one now, only that he was part of them. On one count Eva was right. While he didn't agree with her on the means of the revolution, he did admit that what happened to his family was his fault. Too late, he was no longer afraid to die.

"You're Irgun," he said.

"We all are."

"From the beginning."

"Now."

"What about then?"

"We don't believe in fighting our brothers and sisters." She sounded like Asher.

"So before then."

"We were still Haganah. We're still Haganah."

"And Asher?"

"Asher's Asher."

"What does that mean?"

"Asher's his own man. He likes you, you know. He doesn't like everyone."

"I know. I like him too." The Widow, he called you. But that would start a different argument, one he'd lose.

"You don't trust him."

"I trusted him the other night."

"Touché," she said, toasting Brand. "It's me you don't trust. You know, every night I could cut your throat."

"You mean while you're sleeping and I'm listening to you snore. That's how you'll surprise me."

"Exactly. You'll have no idea until it's over."

"That's how I'd prefer it."

It seemed to be his gift, making her laugh, though in this case he was serious.

Christmas was finally over. The dead season was upon them, the trains from Jaffa running empty. It wasn't worth sitting in the station queue. He followed Pincus and Scheib's advice, sticking to the better hotels, laying for rich Americans, even if it meant the occasional search. Against his instincts, he strewed old rags and oilcans and crumpled lunch bags about his trunk to confuse the dogs. There was nothing in the compartment, only the promise of contraband—enough to hold him. At every checkpoint he practiced his English accent. "What's all this then, eh?" Clever Jossi, everybody's friend. That he wasn't making any money was annoying but ultimately meant nothing. Eventually Asher would call, and Brand's other life would begin again.

When the call finally came, it wasn't from Asher but Fein, throwing off not just Brand but Mrs. Ohanesian, who frowned at the mysterious voice as if Brand should have prepared her. It was Thursday evening. He'd been at Eva's every night that week, yet somehow they knew he was home. He'd forgotten: there were watchers everywhere.

The meeting was in Mekor Baruch, not far from the old-age home. Brand drove Eva and Lipschitz, a mismatched couple, parking on a street lined with scabby sycamores and squat apartment blocks. Here the luckier children of the war swarmed the dusty alleys, playing commando with branches and seed balls, hollering to one another in Polish mixed with Yiddish. Above, their mothers hung boiled laundry from the fire escapes like dull bunting. The coded address Fein had given Brand led to the building most likely to host a secret meeting, a drab Ashkenazi synagogue beside a butcher shop with headless chickens in the window for Sabbath dinner. Before he opened the door, he had a hunch it might be a trap. Why had Fein called? Had something happened to Asher?

Inside, Brand wasn't sure where to go. For a taxi driver, he had no sense of direction. As always, he thought the basement would be the safest place. As if she'd been there before, Eva took the stairs straight to the second floor.

In a small meeting room with a chalkboard on wheels sat Asher, Victor and, in a rumpled seersucker suit, his Star of David and lion tattoo hidden beneath an Oxford shirt, the Sabra.

In the suit he looked more than ever an Arab, the hawk nose and dark skin making the yod-shaped scar above his eye seem even stranger, the mark of fate. He had a boxer's build, a scrappy bantamweight like John Garfield, and Garfield's carelessly tousled hair. He looked like a gangster dressed for a trial. It was hard to believe he'd nearly died just a month ago. Brand realized he was staring and recovered.

"Glad to see you're feeling better."

The man nodded in acknowledgment. To Eva, he nodded significantly, as if in gratitude. Brand recalled him moaning wordlessly in the backseat and wondered if he was a mute. After a minute, Brand realized no one was speaking—not Asher or Victor. Protocol. There would be no introductions.

They all sat around the table waiting for Fein

and Yellin. The chalkboard was sponged clean. Lipschitz took out a pad and began writing. The Sabra waved a hand and he put it away.

From the hall came footfalls, the clash of a door. Fein was alone, and though Brand wanted to ask after Yellin, he waited for someone else to break the silence.

"Close the door," Asher said.

Apparently Yellin wasn't coming, another development Brand didn't like on principle.

The Sabra stood and buttoned his jacket, smoothing his front as if he were going to make a speech. "First, I want to thank you. My friend here tells me how instrumental you were in helping me the other night. I'm indebted to you, and will do my utmost to repay your kindness." He spoke stiffly, as if addressing a crowd. Brand, who had practice, couldn't place the accent— part Spanish, part something else. Maybe French, with its buzzing sibilants. It was possible the Sabra wasn't a Sabra at all.

"I would especially like to thank Miss Eva for the use of her apartment. You're very brave."

*Miss Eva.* She beamed, a star accepting an award.

"I want to thank Jossi for the use of his car. You're very brave as well."

Brand nodded, thinking Asher shouldn't have told him their names. Protocol worked both ways. And what about his sweater?

"You risked your lives to save mine. Don't think I'll forget. Long Live Eretz Israel."

"Long Live Eretz Israel," they echoed.

With that, he sat down and Victor stood up. They made an odd pair, the dark, clean-shaven bantamweight and the ruddy, ginger-bearded giant. How had they met? Brand wondered. Who else was in their cell?

Victor flipped the chalkboard, revealing a diagram—a crude map with train tracks and two parallel roads marked with arrows. As in a geometry problem, the tracks crossed both roads at an angle. Between them, in the center of the tracks, sat a pirate's X for treasure.

"Every Friday the British payroll arrives by the same train."

The plan was ridiculously simple. They were going to blow up the tracks and stick up the train. To Brand the idea seemed like something out of the Wild West, sure to end in a bloody shootout, but no one protested.

Once the train passed the first crossing, they'd blow the tracks behind and ahead of it with mines. With the train trapped, two of them would use the crew as hostages while the others disarmed the guards and blew the safe. They'd use a stolen car, one they could ditch after they'd gotten away, then Jossi would drive them back to the city, the loot safe in the hidden compartment. The payroll was over thirty thousand pounds.

"That's a lot of weapons," Asher said, as if they needed an incentive.

After the substation, Brand expected he'd be part of the assault team, along with Asher, Victor and the Sabra. The Peugeot could hold five. Maybe Fein? Eva and Yellin would handle communications.

They had one week.

"I know that's not a lot of time," Victor said, "but Gideon and I both think you're ready."

"Thank you," Asher said, and as Brand held on to the assumed name, he understood that Gideon and Victor weren't coming with them. They'd be going it alone.

To avoid suspicion, after the meeting was done, they left in shifts. Asher stayed behind with Gideon and Victor to work out the necessary materials. Lipschitz had business in Mahane Yehuda, so he could walk. Fein said he could use a ride.

In the car they were somber, as if right now they were heading out on the mission. They passed the Schneller Barracks and the fields of the orphanage. Brand glanced at the barns and the spindly tower rising in the distance. A moving train was a completely different proposition. Hostages, and guards. Not to mention the safe.

After a mile-long silence, Eva finally spoke. "So, what happened to your buddy Yellin?"

"Nothing," Fein said. "He had a dentist appointment."

# — 5 —

Gideon was Sephardic, a Moroccan whose missionary parents ran a yeshiva in Tangiers. Eva had known all along.

"I couldn't tell you. Believe me, I wanted to. Asher said it was for your own good. We have to be safe."

"You already knew Victor."

"I never said I didn't."

He questioned her like a deceived husband. How well did she know them? How long? She was evasive and outraged, the faithful wife, citing protocol. As he had that first night, he sensed it wasn't the first time Gideon had visited her bed, or Asher. Why was he surprised she was a whore? He was used to Katya, whose past, like his own, was clear as water. He was just a dumb mechanic, he wasn't meant to connive with spies.

"What about the blonde?"

"She's new. Honestly, I have no idea who she is."

" 'Honestly.' "

Her face changed. She pointed to the door. "Get out. Now."

All weekend he stayed away from her place,

working late and eating at the Alaska. In Riga the trials had wrapped, the five men responsible for the massacre hanged, the rest of the city tacitly exonerated—just as he expected, meager consolation. His old life was over, his new one a shambles and a sham. To celebrate, he paced his flat with a glass of Johnnie Walker, bumping his nose against the cold window, leaving a greasy smudge. The humming, stumbling melancholy of solitary drunks. Why was Katya dead and Eva alive? She probably didn't even miss him. She'd probably already hired another driver. The station was so close, he heard the last train from Jaffa laboring up the final grade of Mount Zion, and then his fellow cabbies shuttling passengers into the city, making money. In the crypt his pistols waited, newly oiled. Child of the Great War, survivor of the last, his entire life he'd never pointed a gun at another man, only had them pointed at him. Innocent Brand, the pigeon of history. It was a miracle he'd lived this long.

"Goddamn, yes," he said to his reflection, and was surprised to find his glass empty.

He woke in his clothes, sour-mouthed. At the garage Pincus brought him coffee, hovering like a mother. Greta set him up with an older American couple going to Bethlehem for their anniversary. With everyone on his side, how could he fail?

He wasn't so much afraid as annoyed at the prospect of the mission, as if it were a checkpoint blocking the route to his new life. He could see the reasons for it, and generally agreed wit them, but as the workweek kicked in, he began hoping it would rain on Friday, making the desert impassable for anything but a jeep. Even that would only postpone it.

Tuesday Asher called a meeting for the following evening at the high school. If stopped, they were an amateur drama club working with Eva. Brand thought the idea would please her. Out of habit he swung by to give her a ride, taking the shortcut through the flower market to her gate. The lamp wasn't lit, but when he knocked, there was no answer.

She'd taken the bus. She wanted him to be shocked, and while he was, mildly, he was also flattered that as she schemed, she was thinking of him. Yellin apologized for missing the last meeting but didn't mention the dentist. On a chalkboard Asher ran through the plan, which seemed to Brand both overly complicated and too simple. Asher would meet them with the second car at a kibbutz a few miles from the chosen spot. Brand, Fein and Yellin would watch the hostages while Asher and Lipschitz blew the safe. The car could hold only five of them, so Eva would monitor the escape route from the kibbutz and handle communications. The whole operation was wishful, based on the guards trading the payroll for the hostages. If they refused, would Asher really kill them? From experience Brand was leery of anything with too many moving parts. At least Eva would be safe.

Afterward, she refused a ride home, then, in the parking lot, when it began to rain, changed her mind. She sat in back and spoke only to Fein and Lipschitz, letting Brand know it wasn't a victory. Brand, used to losing, knew it was.

He expected they would make up before the operation. Eventually she'd forgive him, he'd apologize, and they'd go on in their normal, tortured way—or that was how it had worked with Katya. He believed this until two o'clock Thursday afternoon, sitting at the Lions' Gate. Mad as it sounded, in twenty-four hours, inevitable as the sun rising, he would be in the Valley of Ayalon, aiming a gun at a train. Rather than spur him to go see her, the idea made him colder. At this moment, if that was all she cared for him, the hell with her. She should have told him about Gideon in the first place. And yet that night, listening for Mrs. Ohanesian's phone to ring, he debated getting dressed and going down to the Peugeot. Their first night together, when she was just The Widow, he'd felt her husband and Katya in the room with them, their presence both mournful and a comfort, as if this was what was left to them. Only a fool would sacrifice that last consolation to pride, yet here he was.

In the morning a guilty vestige of the feeling remained, like a faintly remembered dream, but it was too late. He unlocked the Peugeot and slipped into the cemetery for his pistols, the old and the new both wrapped in oilcloth. Popping the trunk, he pictured Mrs. Ohanesian watching him from her window. With all the rain, the hidden compartment smelled of mildew. He set the bundle down as if it might explode.

Eva was the first one he picked up, giving them some time alone. She wasn't used to being up so early and looked tired around the eyes. As always, she'd thrown herself into the role, wearing a powder-blue headscarf, a white blouse and khaki pants like a Youth League kibbutznik, as if, with her soft hands and mascara, she might fit in. Before the checkpoint, he apologized.

"I know," she said. "I was sick all day yesterday."

"I wanted to come by last night."

"You should have."

"I was being an idiot."

This they could agree on.

"You'll be careful," she asked.

"That's me, Mr. Careful."

"Please don't joke." She gave him a helpless face, and he understood he couldn't die. He reached a hand over the seat for her to squeeze.

"Don't worry."

"Why not?"

"Gideon said it himself, I'm very brave."

"I'm not," she said.

"That's not true."

As they curled through the suburbs, gathering the cell one at a time like a dire carpool, she moved to the front. Lipschitz was the last, wearing a black frock coat too heavy for the weather. Beneath it he had a Sten machine gun Fein and Yellin admired as if it were a grandchild.

They took the Jaffa Road for the coast, passing the bus station and the reservoir, leaving the city behind. The desert outskirts were Arab territory. On both sides chalk-white villages dotted the cliffs like hawks' nests commanding the valley and its ancient trade route. This was the land of the Canaanites, occupied by the Philistines and Babylonians and Romans before the Ottomans and the British. Now the main population, again, after the foreign invaders had retreated, was lizards and scorpions. Pincus and Scheib had warned Brand never to take a fare here at night. At first, like Eva's stories of the riots, their advice seemed overwrought. Now he saw it as common sense. There were no call boxes out here, no law.

"Damn it," he said. "I forgot my bandana."

"So did I," Yellin confessed.

"They'll have some where we're going," Fein said.

"You can use my babushka," Eva told Brand, taking it off and refolding it on her lap for him. He would be her champion.

The road took them through Bab el-Wad, a notorious stronghold of the Arab Legion. Brand slowed as if the traffic police were laying for him. It was the Moslem holy day and the market-place was closed, the main street deserted. Only a beggar in a soiled kaftan stopped to stare at the novelty of a cab full of Jews, and at the edge of town Brand sped up again.

After Latrun they descended, breasting the Judean Hills before dropping into the Valley of Ayalon, the view before them endless, stretching to the coastal plain. Miles ahead on the desert floor, like smoke from a fire, another car kicked up a tail of dust. So far off, with no wind, it was impossible to tell if it was coming toward them or headed for Tel Aviv. If it was a patrol, there was no way to disguise their approach. Brand could see them being stopped and Lipschitz opening up with the Sten, the jeep or armored car raking them before they could get out of their seats. If it was an armored car, it might be better to go cross-country and try to outrun them. Against a jeep they had no chance.

"What's that?" Eva asked, pointing to something by the roadside.

From a distance it looked like the frame of a tent or Quonset hut, maybe a burnt-out gas station or café. As they neared, it solidified into the hulk of a bus rusted the color of dried blood.

"That's been there forever," Yellin said. "They're dead ducks going uphill."

The directions Asher had given him took them off the highway and along a dry wadi running back into the foothills. There was no road, only a loose consensus of tire tracks. He craned over the wheel, the Peugeot dipping into ruts and bumping over stones like a launch in choppy water. He figured they had enough people to push if they got stuck. There were no trees for cover, just cactus and scrub, and he was relieved when they were finally out of sight of the highway.

As they climbed into the hills, he imagined Asher had been stopped, the fake plates discovered, the mines. Without the second car they'd have to turn back. Without Asher, the cell would dissolve and Brand would be free, a coward without a home or a people. Was that what he wanted? Why did he have to fight so hard to overcome his worst instincts?

"I see it," Eva said, and there it was, around the bend.

Kibbutz Ramat Avraham sat atop a knoll like a colonial outpost, ringed on all sides, like police headquarters, with barbed wire. Over the compound rose a shiny new water tower crowned with a Star of David flag. On its catwalk paced a pair of men with sniper rifles. The gate was barricaded by a truck liberated from the Italian army, still flying the tricolor on its canvas side, which looked moth-eaten, but, as they slowed, proved to be pocked with bullet holes. At a signal from the catwalk, the truck pulled up enough for Brand to sneak by, then when he was through, backed up again, sealing them in. Inside the wire, the buildings were makeshift, a canvas mess hall and barracks on raw wooden platforms spaced around a bald parade ground, and with the panic of a man held underwater too long, Brand wanted out.

During the war he'd lived in tents like these, stifling in the summer and freezing in the winter, sharing his straw mattress with rats. He lined up for roll call morning and evening and ate off tin plates, licking the rusty metal to get the last dab of porridge. When someone died, they divvied up his Red Cross package and had a party. After the guard they called Nosey killed Koppelman, Brand let someone else have his share. He was through being a beast, a vow he'd break the next day, and the next— the rest of his life, he'd thought. He'd die before he lived like that again.

Asher saved him, striding across the parade ground with his valise as if he'd called a cab.

"Morning," he said, leaning in the window, turning a smile on everyone. "No problems, I take it."

"None."

"Good. We're actually a little early. Pull around to that shed and I'll meet you there."

Brand took the drive at a crawl, their progress followed by lookouts on the catwalk. Instead of disappointed, he was grateful to no longer be in charge. Asher made the operation seem possible, as if he could do it himself. To Brand it didn't make sense. Though he didn't know Asher, he believed in him.

The other car was a stake truck with an official-looking Palestine Railways logo on the doors.

"It is," Asher confirmed, without elaborating. In the bed were picks and shovels and a pair of wheelbarrows. He had white kaftans and keffiyehs for everyone, and makeup for their faces. The plan had changed slightly. They'd still blow the tracks, but just in one spot, and now they'd also be repairing them. The engineer would stop to see what the problem was, Asher would climb into the cab, and like that they'd have the train.

"Why do we have to blow up the tracks?" Yellin asked. "Why can't we just be working on them?"

"We *want* to blow up the tracks," Asher said. "Ideally we'd blow up the train if we had time, but we don't."

Eva helped them with the makeup. Lipschitz made a hilarious Arab, with his moon face and glasses. Lipschitz of the desert. Fein and Yellin could have passed for falafel vendors, Asher a sheikh. Brand, with his green eyes and blond hair, looked like a burn victim. The dimple in his chin itched. Eva straightened his keffiyeh and did a last touch-up of his nose. She put a finger to her lips and pressed it to his.

"Be careful."

"I will."

"Listen to Asher. Watch what he does."

It was time. She let him go, and as he settled into the driver's seat, fixing the mirrors so he could see, he wondered how many comrades she'd told to be careful. Did it matter? He still had her babushka, even if he no longer needed it.

Asher and Lipschitz sat in the cab, Fein and Yellin behind them in the bed with the tools. Asher balanced the valise on his knees, holding it with both hands. They waved goodbye to Eva and set off across the parade ground. There must have been an important meeting, because the kibbutzniks, invisible till now, were streaming out of the mess tent, a khaki mass of suntanned young men and women dedicated to an agrarian, egalitarian homeland. Brand couldn't imagine living here, captive, under constant attack. Having barely survived his own brush with collectivism, he didn't share their ideals, even as he admired their resolve. They all stopped to watch the stolen truck go, waving as if wishing them luck, and he understood this was Asher's doing. He was following protocol, for everyone's sake. Now that they were Arabs, they could safely be seen. They waved back, the Italian truck pulled up, and they were outside the wire.

The stake truck liked the makeshift road even less than the Peugeot had. In back, the shovels clattered as they dropped into holes, Fein and Yellin hanging on to the sides like seasick greenhorns hugging thc rails. At his last work camp Brand had taken care of a fleet of diesels with the same sluggish three-speed. Afraid of getting stuck, he kept to first gear as they followed the sandy wadi, the engine protesting. Once on the highway, he shifted up, and Fein and Yellin took shelter behind the cab.

The sun was higher, flattening shadows, bleaching the valley. Though it was cold, liquid ripples of heat played over the road. The distant smoke they'd seen on the plain was gone. Here there was nothing—a crow jabbing at something in the dust, a tin cross commemorating a pile of stones, a signpost with a pitted arrow pointing off across the desert. Asher opened his valise and unfolded a map covered with scribbles. Brand was too busy driving to read it. Between them sat Lipschitz with his machine gun under his kaftan, his glasses smudged with makeup. Where did he get the Sten, and had he used it before? Again, Brand had underestimated him.

"You don't have to go so fast," Asher said, and Brand let up on the pedal.

"Are we almost there?"

"It should be right up here, if this is right."

Had he not cased the crossing? Someone must have, probably the kibbutzniks, since they knew the area.

"There," Asher said, and Brand slowed until he could see the lollipop marker with the railway logo. When he turned off the highway, the front end dipped and he heard Yellin swear.

"About a mile," Asher said.

Before he could put the map away, they saw the tracks—or the telephone lines attending them, stretching to the horizon in both directions. At a distance, the grade was noticeable, a steady climb into the hills, though as they drew closer, bouncing over the ruts, the valley seemed absolutely flat. The tail of dust that gave the Peugeot away didn't matter here. They were a railway crew in a railway truck, and by the time anyone suspected otherwise, it would be too late.

The tracks sat atop a raised berm along which ran a goat path, the churned earth in the middle darker, the fringes holding hoofprints.

"Go left," Asher said. "In a half mile there

should be a culvert that goes under the tracks."

It was there they stopped and got out. After traveling all morning they were stiff. Fein fell getting out of the bed, knocking off his keffiyeh.

"Next time I'm driving," Yellin said.

"Leave the radio on." Asher pointed toward the hills. "They can see us, in case anything happens."

Brand squinted, trying to find the water tower, but the sun was in his eyes. He waved to Eva anyway.

Asher called them together—to go over the plan, Brand thought. Instead he had them set aside their weapons and showed them how to rig the mine. Today they were using gelignite, and as they watched him pack it into an old tobacco tin, Brand remembered the high school and decided Asher was a teacher. He gave Lipschitz the job of crimping the fuse, then, live mine in hand, led them to the culvert. The second lesson was tamping—using the materials at hand to direct the force of the explosion. By digging a hole under the tie, they'd not only blow up the tracks but collapse the culvert, which would actually take longer to repair.

"Think damage," Asher said, handing the shovel back to Fein.

They had to wait, gathered by the open door of the cab for the radio to let them know the train had left the station in Ramleh. The code word was Cunningham, the British high commissioner, and there it was at the top of the news, eliciting a cheer.

Lipschitz was given the honor. Asher held the fuse for him while the rest of them peeked from behind the truck.

Lipschitz scampered down the berm, making them laugh. Asher came strolling after him, checking his watch. He joined them, counting out loud: "Twenty-four, twenty-five, twenty-six . . ." He stopped when he got to thirty and cocked his head, listening.

"Maybe you—" Yellin said, and was drowned out by the report.

Once, in Naples, Brand had been standing on the docks when a crane lost its counterweight. The crane was five stories tall, the counterweight ten thousand pounds, multiplied by a pulley system. Over the years the braided wire cable holding it had corroded, unraveling strand by strand, weakening until, in an instant, it let go. Though he was a ship's length away, he felt like he'd been punched in the chest, and for several minutes couldn't stop shaking.

This wasn't a surprise, but still made him cringe. The blast seemed to go on a long time, rolling across the desert, echoing off the hills, leaving an isolated, high-pitched whining in his ears. Rocks and clods of dirt rained down around them, hopping off the hood of the truck like hail.

"Let's take a look," Asher said, waving to show it was safe.

The ends of the track were bent and blackened, the section between them gone, atomized by the release of energy. If the culvert hadn't collapsed, as Asher had hoped, it was badly cracked. They celebrated, shaking their heads as if they never expected it to work. Brand laughed, but thought: That's the easy part.

"Five minutes," Asher said, and they hurried to take their places, pushing the empty wheelbarrows up the berm and lifting them onto the tracks. They filled them with dirt, a feeble barricade, then leaned on their shovels like a real crew taking a break. Fein's keffiyeh was cockeyed. Like a valet, Yellin straightened it. From the truck Asher brought a red flag no larger than a pillowcase. As they stood in the lucid sunlight, peering into the shimmering distance, he briefed them a final time. The plan was to walk the engineer back to the mail car, disarm the guards and blow the safe. No one gets off. Show your weapons so they know you mean business. Brand thought he was getting ahead of himself. First they had to stop the train.

As the minutes passed and nothing happened, Brand imagined it wasn't coming, that it had broken down or derailed or, by mad coincidence, another outfit was right now holding it up. Then he saw the smoke.

Asher nodded. They all saw it.

It was just a smudge—it might have been a car—that gradually resolved into a dot. How slowly it approached, without sound, a dark blot around a wavering headlamp, bright even in the sunlight. As it drew closer, the engine took shape, the black boiler and open cab and matching tender. Smoke gushed from the stack, hung suspended above the coaches in a thick plume, a crosswind thinning it, pushing a sooty cloud over the desert.

At their feet the rails sang, faintly at first, then insistent, a steely shivering like a knife being sharpened on a wheel. Through his kaftan Brand touched the butt of his pistol to make sure it was there. Beside him Fein dug into the berm and threw another shovel of dirt into the wheel-barrow. Yellin took his cue and did the same.

They could hear the engine drumming, gathering speed to make the grade, the rhythmic clicking of the wheels filling the air. By now the engineer would have spotted the truck and wondered why they were on the tracks, yet didn't slow. How long did it take a train to stop?

On it came, growing. Though Brand saw locomotives every day at the station, they were at rest, tamed. Here, at full bore, its power seemed elemental, barely controlled. The noise surrounded them, overwhelming. Brand prepared to run. When the engine derailed, it would take the rest of the train with it, the whole thing sliding sideways like a snake off a rock.

Asher stood in the middle of the tracks, waving the flag in long arcs above his head like a signal-man hailing another ship. The train kept on, bearing down on him, the pistons shuttling, until finally, as if it had received his message, the engine relented. The whistle shrieked a warning, shocking Brand's heart, the brakes caught and the wheels ground against the rails, squealing, steel on steel, bowing a long, drawn-out note. The engine slowed, chuffing, coasting till it loomed close over Asher, and with a lurch, stopped, its boiler hissing.

Asher planted the flag between the ties, walked over to the ladder and climbed into the cab.

The other four dug, still pretending to be workers. Brand listened for gunshots. He thought Lipschitz should have gone with Asher, but it was too late now. The train idled like a sleeping beast, bleeding off steam.

The engineer climbed down, followed by the fireman. They stood with their hands clasped behind their heads. From the ladder, Asher waved Lipschitz over. He ran, holding the Sten high across his chest. Brand, who'd pegged him for a scholar or an artist, was surprised at how fast he was, though it made sense. He was by far the youngest of them.

Asher dropped down and waved his pistol, the

signal for them to break out their weapons. He had his keffiyeh wrapped around his head like a bandit, only his eyes visible.

Brand arranged his the same way and drew his pistol. Fein had a long-barreled revolver like his Parabellum, Yellin a nickel-plated snub-nose.

Asher and Lipschitz took the engineer and left them the fireman, a red-haired, red-cheeked Scot with yellow rodent's teeth. Fat, in patched over-alls, he was sweating and kept taking a hand off his head to wipe his brow. "Sorry," he said, then did it again.

They weren't supposed to talk. Yellin gestured with his gun for him to walk ahead of them. Brand followed, his finger on the trigger guard so there was no chance it would go off. They were supposed to fire their weapons only if absolutely necessary, a rule Brand clung to. He'd thought the gun would make him feel powerful. Instead, it magnified his weakness. If the fireman took off running, would he wait for Yellin or Fein to shoot him? Was that any better than shooting him him-self?

As Asher had said, there were only two coaches. Between the three of them they could cover all the doors. Most of the passengers had drawn their shades, but a curious few glared out at them. Yellin had the fireman lie flat on the ground, pointing his gun at his back, and Brand thought of Nosey making him and Koppelman grovel in the snow just to get them wet. It had been a game to Nosey, one Koppelman finally tired of. The little German tormented them at random, according to his whim. It could have been Brand on the floor of the machine shop that morning—a thought that crossed his mind as, with the rest of the prisoners, he watched Nosey stomping Koppelman's head long after Koppelman had stopped moving. The idea that he was watching someone kill another person—that Koppelman had died—wasn't a surprise. What was more important was not drawing attention to himself, though soon enough, with Koppelman gone, Brand became his favorite target, and for a long time—even now, if he was honest—he blamed Koppelman.

Farther down the train, Asher held his pistol to the engineer's temple. After the briefest of negotiations, the door of the mail car slid open. Lipschitz covered the guards as they threw their Thompsons out and clambered down. Once he'd collected their weapons and everyone was on the ground, Asher climbed inside.

As they waited for the charge to go off, the faint burring of an engine reached them. Fein and Yellin looked to Brand with concern. It reverberated all around them, swelling, a thrumming like another train, growing louder and louder. It wasn't possible—Asher would have checked the schedule—and then Fein pointed to the sky. A plane. It took Brand a few seconds to find the dark cross, high up: not a Spitfire sent to strafe them but a fat transport droning for the coast.

The fireman swabbed his forehead, and Yellin kicked his foot.

Inside his keffiyeh Brand was sweating, his hot breath caught in the cloth. He watched the rear door of the second coach, stealing glances at the windows. Having picked up his share of passengers from the station, he'd wager there were soldiers onboard, possibly armed. As he searched the windows for a flash of army khaki or RAF blue, a woman's face stopped him, at once strange and familiar, the striking cheekbones and straight nose of an heiress, bright hair tucked under a beret. With the glare, he thought it might be a trick of the light, but on second look he wasn't mistaken. Though he'd seen her only twice, both times in a kind of costume, he knew her the way he knew Victor or Gideon, indelibly. Peering out at him with the hauteur of Garbo was the blonde from the Eden Hotel.

He was trying to decide if she was Asher's plant when the mail car exploded, sending broken boards pinwheeling skyward, peppering the hostages with debris. He saw Lipschitz drop his gun and grab his throat with both hands, stagger sideways a few steps and fall to his knees.

Brand ran over and picked up the Sten, pointing it at the engineer and the guards, who were sitting up, bleeding from a dozen cuts, their uniforms torn. Flaming paper snowed down around them.

"Lie down!" Brand threatened, and they did. "Hands on your head!"

A splinter the size of a steak knife stuck from Lipschitz's neck. He'd lost his glasses and his keffiyeh had unraveled, giving away the masquerade. He looked at Brand without recognition.

"Can you hear me?"

Lipschitz nodded, as if afraid to speak.

Brand pried his fingers apart. Where the splinter entered, it was no thicker than a pencil. Brand gripped it tight and yanked. He was ready for a gush of blood, but only a little welled up, overflowing the hole. It had missed the jugular. He stanched the wound with the keffiyeh and made Lipschitz hold it in place.

"I can't see," Lipschitz said.

His glasses were intact, a few feet away. Brand hooked them over his ears. Lipschitz looked around, dazed, as if he were just waking up.

"Go back to the truck," Brand ordered, then had to steer him in the right direction, pointing at Fein to take him.

Something must have gone wrong with the charge. One wall of the car was gone, and part of the roof, giving Brand a view of steamer trunks and packing cases and shipping crates piled like a child's building blocks. With all the smoke he didn't see Asher, and, backing around, keeping the gun trained on the hostages, made his way up the berm. The floor was at eye level, and, like the crates, badly splintered. He could see only the rear of the safe, a lacquered black box taller than he was. From inside came a busy rustling, like someone stuffing a mattress with leaves.

"Are you all right?" he called.

"I'm all right," Asher called.

Brand still didn't see him. He sidled around to the other side of the hole for a better look, all the while eyeing the hostages. The door of the safe was open.

"Do you need help?"

Asher peered around the door. He was still wearing his keffiyeh. "Here."

He slid a canvas bag across the floor to Brand, then followed, carrying another over his shoulder. Miraculously, he was untouched, his kaftan pristine.

"Where's Lipschitz?"

"He had a splinter." Brand nudged the gun at the hostages. "What do we do with them?"

"Leave them. Come on."

The bag was heavy, jostling against his back as they ran. It was farther than he remembered. Passing the coaches, he felt the blonde watching them. Eva probably had them in her binoculars.

Everywhere, observers. Fein and Yellin covered them, then retreated.

Lipschitz was sitting in the truck, listening to the radio. There'd been no word. Brand jammed the shift in gear and aimed for the highway, leaving behind the wheelbarrows and shovels. The bags sat at Asher's feet. They hadn't fired a shot, only blown up a railcar on His Majesty's Service.

The temptation was to gun it, but Brand was careful, aware of Fein and Yellin in back.

"Thank you," Lipschitz said when they were on the main road. "I thought I was going to die."

"I thought you were too."

"What happened?" Asher asked, and Lipschitz told him, making it sound like Brand had rescued him.

"You saved us," Asher said.

"I wouldn't say that."

"You did," Lipschitz said.

Back at the kibbutz, Fein and Yellin agreed, Brand was the hero.

"You should have seen him," Fein told Eva as she swabbed off their makeup.

"I did," she said.

The take was twenty-eight thousand pounds. It barely fit in the compartment. Asher would stay behind and get rid of the truck. He saw them off in the shed, leaning in the window of the Peugeot as he had that morning.

"Well done, everyone. Jossi, good job." He squeezed Brand's arm and stood back.

Later, going over the day with Eva asleep beside him, it was that moment he returned to, not his decision to leave his post and help Lipschitz. That had been a reflex. Anyone would have done the same, except the Brand who claimed to be Koppelman's friend and then let him die. The camps had made him selfish and doubtful. To have someone think well of him now was uncomfortable, because he knew the truth. He'd come to Jerusalem to change, to reclaim himself. Like Eva giving him her babushka, Asher squeezing his arm gave him hope. After being an animal for so long, he didn't think he'd ever be a man again, but if they believed in him, maybe it was possible.

The other memory he revisited was picking up the Sten and ordering the hostages to lie down on the ground. Hands on your head, he'd said, as if it came naturally. As soon as the words were out of his mouth, he knew where they'd come from. He barked it, more threat than command. The familiar intonation shocked him, like a pet phrase of his mother's bubbling up, and behind the machine gun, as now, in bed, remembering, Brand cringed. Coincidence or not, it seemed wrong that at his most heroic he sounded exactly like Nosey.

He thought they'd proved themselves with the train job, yet for weeks Asher had nothing for them. Radio silence, Radio Cairo. Winter was over, the desert beginning to bloom. The cemetery smelled of jasmine and lavender. Brand put away his sweater and left his window open all day. Instead of going out on missions, hc drove the Peugeot and listened to the news as other cells attacked the power station and the central prison and, one night when he was only a few streets over so that he ended up getting stuck at a roadblock, the Palestine Broadcasting Service on Queen Melisande's Way, taking heavy casualties. He was at once enraged at the waste and jealous of their daring.

Having survived everything that had gone wrong on the train job and come away with the loot, he now saw it as a great success. He'd forgotten how he felt hearing the plane that might have been a Spitfire (it wasn't), and watching Lipschitz clutch his neck and pitch forward as if he'd been killed (he hadn't). He knew nothing of the PBS operation except rumors passed around the queue, but with the pride of the newly triumphant he was certain they could have done better.

Eva had a new lunchtime client at the King David. He was a minister of business affairs, a Jew, and married, an easy mark. A strange case, Eva said. Very carefully he hung up his tie and jacket and slacks, fit his socks and sock garters into his shoes and shut the closet door, as if to protect them, yet the entire time he wore his undershirt and shorts. Lately she had a habit of denigrating her clients—out of loyalty, Brand supposed. He wished she wouldn't say anything. He already pictured too much.

Waiting for her, he noted the comings and goings of the Secretariat. The hotel had three restaurants and two bars, and lunch was a busy time. The clerks and stenographers and switchboard operators brought their own, filling the wicker chairs on the rear terrace and the benches of the rose garden, eating sandwiches and left-overs off their laps, but the main dining room and the grill room and the Arab Lounge were elaborately decorated stages where power brokers from Tripoli to Teheran met on neutral ground to finalize deals over pink gins and bloody filets. Brand knew them by their cars. Here, among the high command's armored Humbers and the tycoons' sleek limousines, the blonde's Daimler wouldn't raise an eyebrow. The drive was lined with majestic prewar

Bugattis and brand-new Rolls bought with oil money. He'd seen Montgomery's former second in command and King Faisal of Iraq walking hand in hand like lovers, heads bowed, discussing the business of empire, and Clark Gable stopping on his way to India, and the great Heifetz, come to play a benefit for the Jewish National Fund. Once, as Brand was reading the *Post*, the high commis-sioner had crossed not three feet in front of his bumper. Like the waiters and cigarette girls at the Kilimanjaro, the doormen and valets all knew Eva, and soon the Peugeot. All they had to do was fill the trunk with TNT, set a timer and slip out the back.

There were targets everywhere, yawning opportunities. The military courts, the YMCA, the train station. Instead, he gave his unsuspecting fares the tour of the seven gates and pointed them toward the orange juice stand owned by Scheib's cousin.

With their share of the money, he and Eva could have gone anywhere and started over.

"I had to fight to get here," she said. "I have to fight to stay here. Why would I give up now?"

They had no say anyway. The money went to Tel Aviv in a load of potash. Brand knew she was right, but sometimes, sitting in the queue outside the King David, he daydreamed of a place in the woods like his grandfather's dacha, with a stone hearth and a thatch-roofed shed in the garden where he could cobble together bird-houses. Sentimental Brand, heir to the Romantics, lover of fireflies and white nights. Why did he suddenly want to blow everything up?

Others were. The radar station near Caesarea, where the *Eastern Star* had docked. The oil depot outside of Tulkarm. Eighteen RAF planes at three separate airfields. Alone in the Peugeot, Brand listened to the damage reports from these operations with undisguised envy, as if he'd thought of them first.

Eva celebrated the bombings but hated the curfews that inevitably followed. Like Mrs. Ohanesian, she complained about hoarders, meanwhile squirreling away enough food, cigarettes and cognac to hole up for a month. Brand didn't keep much in his flat, and once was stranded with nothing to eat but sardines and old soda crackers. The bombings also meant he was stopped more often, the car searched more thoroughly, but then for several weeks things were quiet, and the Tommies jotted down his badge number and waved him through.

Jerusalem in the spring. The walls of the Old City weren't golden but the color of ripe wheat. Beards of hyssop grew from the seams, dotted with tiny white flowers. The sky reminded Brand of the Baltic in summer, its blue endlessness, making sandcastles on the beach with Giggi, gathering driftwood for that night's fire as if it were a game. With the weather, it was hard to remember they were at war. In Rehavia the almond trees were blooming. The cafés moved their tables outside, and in the evenings Zion Square was full of students. Brand took Eva to see *Caesar and Cleopatra*, which made her weep, and *Confidential Agent*, which made her laugh. She loved Vivien Leigh. Bacall wasn't an actress, anyone could see she was a model from the way she held her head. Back at Eva's flat they had a nightcap under the stars in her little roof garden, Benny Goodman tootling from the other room, and slept with the windows open. In the middle of a dream, walking the streets of Riga, he woke to a mournful baying—a lonely dog, he thought, and then it was joined by another, and another, an entire pack. Outside the Dung Gate, in the Valley of Hinnom, the jackals were hunting.

One night they were coming back after seeing *And Then There Were None* when the curfew siren wound up, blaring its soaring warning. Along Agrippas Street, people scurried as if it were an air raid. Brand tried the radio, but there was nothing. By the time they reached the Zion Gate, the checkpoint would be in effect, and rather than run the risk, he proposed they stay at his place.

"If you don't mind."

"Won't your landlady be scandalized?"

"No," Brand said, though Mrs. Ohanesian was

scandalized by jazz and strange voices on the phone.

"I've been wondering why you never let me see it. It can't be that bad."

"It's a room. There's not much to it."

"I bet it's spotless."

"Hardly." While it was clean, he was afraid she would see it as bare, the lair of a sad bachelor.

When they pulled in, Mrs. Ohanesian's bay window was lit. They would just have to brazen it out—another operation they hadn't planned for. On the porch Brand gently opened the door and let Eva go up first, shielding her from behind, but there was no disguising their footsteps, and once they were in his room she was directly below them. He was sure he would hear about it soon enough.

Eva stopped just inside the door, as if waiting for him. Rather than turn on the naked ceiling bulb and expose his empty walls, he shuffled to the head of his bed and groped for the radio, the music and soft orange light of the dial filling the room. She went to the open window and looked down over the cemetery. Even with the curfew there would be some couples, and he closed the window as if against a breeze.

"Tea or scotch?"

"Tea, please. It's very cozy."

"I told you it wasn't much." He lit the Primus stove and offered her his one chair. The song they were playing was lush with strings and a low, smoky clarinet. A sad Billie Holiday rasped. *Yesterdays. Yesterdays. Days I knew as happy, sweet, sequestered days.* Eva had taken to wearing her hair like Veronica Lake, a dark curtain hiding one side of her face, and the lighting was kind. This is what she must have looked like, and before he could banish the thought, she leaned in and kissed him deeply, staying close after they broke.

"I don't usually go to men's rooms."

"No?"

"No. They come to me. I like your room. It's like you."

"How's that?"

"It's honest."

He wasn't sure that was true, or what she was trying to imply by it, but her lips were nearly touching his ear, her warm breath tickling his neck, and he knew better than to argue. She kissed him and twisted around to turn off the stove, which was fine with him. He didn't want tea anyway.

Katya would come to him later, not as an angel but a memory—a day on the same beach he and Giggi went to every summer as children, a family vacation, the two of them lying there, letting the sun melt into their skin as the waves broke and foamed, the undertow dragging back pebbles. At the end of the day there was no need to speak. They threw their towels over their shoulders and walked back hand in hand to the cottage, where the swollen doors wouldn't close, so that, though they were married, they had to wait till the whole house was asleep to make love. Like Giggi on the beach, the memory had come unbidden. To Brand the meaning was unclear. Those effortless hours lying beside her might have been the happiest of his life. What was this, then? The problem, as always, was that he was still alive.

In the morning they learned the reason for the curfew. Thirty Irgun fighters dressed as soldiers stole an army truck, finessed their way onto the main base at Sarafand and filled it with weapons from the armory before the British realized what was happening. The Irgun managed to escape with the truck, but in the gun battle two of them were badly hurt. Two female first-aid workers were driving them to a safe house in Tel Aviv when an armored car stopped them. The four were charged with crimes against the state. The men would certainly get the death penalty.

Neither of them recognized the names, but they wouldn't. He'd have to see their photos in the *Post*.

For once Brand wasn't jealous. It might have happened to him, driving Gideon. It might have been him instead of Koppelman. He'd come to understand: so much of life was luck.

"You know they won't let them do it," Eva said. "How will they stop it?"

"I don't know, but they will. The Old Man will figure something out."

She meant the Irgun's mastermind, Begin, fighting the revolution from a garden apartment in Tel Aviv. Too important to risk firing a weapon, he arranged arms deals with the Czechs and ordered assassinations, his young wife smuggling out his instructions in a baby carriage. He'd survived hunting season, when the Haganah and the British had joined forces. Now, for better or worse, he was their leader. Eva was right. His code was simple, lifted from scripture. An eye for an eye—a price the civilized British weren't willing to pay.

The curfew lifted, they were free to leave, but dawdled over their tea, as if they wouldn't be here again. By daylight the place looked as spare as a monk's cell, his few possessions meager. He wished he'd hung something on the walls.

"How do you live without a mirror?"

"There's one in the bathroom."

"That's not what I mean."

"I already know what I look like."

She thought he could use some curtains. He didn't say the blinds worked fine. Before leaving, he opened the window. Below, placed like an offering on one crypt, lay a pair of khaki skivvies.

They were careful on the stairs and closing

the door, making a clean getaway, and then, as he was backing up, Mrs. Ohanesian came out on the porch and stood with her arms folded, as if seeing them off. Brand waved, neighborly. Mrs. Ohanesian didn't.

"I'd say she was fairly scandalized," Eva said.

"She'll get over it," Brand said, with a bravado that surprised him. One holdup and he was turning into a gangster.

He saw her to her door in the Quarter as if it were a date. Her lunchtime client was tomorrow, so her day was free. He had to drive.

"What about tonight?" he asked.

"Are you making me an offer?"

"I guess I am."

Thanks to the Sarafand raid, there were searches at the checkpoints, and another curfew, an excuse to stay the night, drinking cognac and stargazing from her roof garden. Pleasantly tight, he admired her thriving grape arbor and her potted geraniums and decided what he needed was a plant—an idea she liked. They'd pick something out together, something that fit him; she knew exactly where to go. The next morning they both remembered, but they had work, and put it off until the weekend—Shushan Purim, an extra day of celebration because Jerusalem, like the Persian capital, was a walled city. The streets were full of costumed revelers bringing hamantaschen and sugared almonds to friends, students with blue boxes collecting door-to-door for the National Fund. Brand and Eva joined the parade, and at the end of the night there was no question where they'd sleep. Her flat was right there, her bed a double, and no nosy landlady to watch them come and go.

Though she'd never admit it, it was she, not Mrs. Ohanesian, who was scandalized. While Eva would ultimately help him pick out a flowering Christmas cactus—their little joke—she never saw the place of honor he gave it on his night table beside his radio, and though he would have happily put up a mirror and curtains for her, there was no reason, and his room remained the same as it had been when he first moved in with just his sea bag. Sometimes at night when a Billie Holiday song came on, he remembered her being there as if it were a dream. There was the chair she sat in. Here was the pillow where she laid her head. It was futile, like trying to recall his mother's voice or that afternoon with Katya, yet he returned to it again and again, sometimes even when he was with her, making him question his happiness.

With the sun, the tourists were back, and the days dragged, one snapshot after another. For all its marvels, Jerusalem was small. Only months ago the view from the Mount of Olives—the real-life version of his mother's lithograph—had thrilled him. Now he leaned against a fender and blew smoke rings at the Dome of the Rock.

Across the Old City, rosy in a sea of white, stood the King David. Right now the man might be sipping his coffee and looking out his window at him. Brand imagined him watching the clock all morning, counting the minutes, and then, because she was prompt, ever the professional, the delicious panic of knowing she was walking through the lobby, she was getting on the elevator, her silk lingerie slippery beneath her clothes. The man would have to duck his colleagues in the halls, draw the blinds against the light. How expensive was the room, and how did he keep it a secret from his wife? Those rolled socks and garters. Brand was at once jealous and sneeringly superior. Yet every Monday he was the one eating lunch in his car, waiting for him to finish.

According to the *Post*, the two prisoners were heroes, martyrs to the cause. The Irgun's handbills said the British would be pronouncing a death sentence on their own troops if they carried through with it. A life for a life.

To help overthrow their fascist Nazi British oppressors, Brand washed his car. The black showed the dust, and with the heat the trash in the trunk was beginning to stink. In the driveway, under the baleful eye of Mrs. Ohanesian, he globbed on wax and rubbed it in with a chamois mitt Pincus had lent him, until he could see his face. A day later the dust was back. At least the trunk was clean.

He drove Greeks to the Greek Colony and Americans to the American Colony and Russians to the Russian Compound. He lugged luggage and made change, sold rolls of film and counted his tips. The tourists wore him out. Where was Jesus buried? Who had the best ruins?

Just as he'd resigned himself to the grind, Asher resurfaced.

"It's your friend," Mrs. Ohanesian said. At first Brand thought she meant Eva. She closed her door as if to give him privacy.

"This is Mr. Lipschitz," Asher said. "I have a doctor's appointment at the British hospital tomorrow morning, and I need a ride. Can you pick me up at nine thirty?"

Brand didn't know the code, but played along. "Of course. Where are you located?"

Strauss Street was just off the Street of the Prophets, five minutes at most from the hospital, and after he'd hung up and Mrs. Ohanesian retreated to her piano, he climbed the stairs, biting the inside of his cheek, wondering what it all meant.

The intrigue only deepened the next morning when not Asher but Lipschitz was waiting for him outside the Strauss Health Center with a white bandage taped to his neck and a manila folder in one hand. As always, he was in black, and Brand smiled, picturing him in the kaftan.

Like a rabbi, he kept his hat on in the car.

"What are we doing?" Brand asked.

"I have a doctor's appointment." He pointed to his neck.

"How is it?"

Lipschitz shrugged. "It could be worse. Go around to the emergency entrance."

At the foot of the drive, unexpectedly, there was a checkpoint, complete with a jeep and an armored car. A pair of Tommies moved a tangle of barbed wire to let an ambulance through. Suddenly everything made sense. The prisoners were there.

"Why didn't you tell me?"

"I thought you knew."

"How would I know?" Brand said. "Nobody tells me anything."

"It's all right," Lipschitz said, holding up the folder. "I've got an appointment."

"A real one."

"That's what I'm telling you."

It was real, irrefutable as Brand's badge. After a cursory once-over, the soldier gave Lipschitz back his folder and waved the barbed wire aside. Brand tried to pull in behind the ambulance, but an Arab policeman stopped him.

"Sir, I'm afraid you can't stop here."

"I'm just dropping a patient off."

"Please, sir. You're welcome to drop him down there. This is for emergencies only."

"Thank you," Brand said, nodding courteously, and moved on.

A minute later, after Lipschitz had gone in, the policeman rousted him again. They needed to keep this area clear. He was welcome to wait farther down.

"Thank you," Brand said.

As Jossi, he'd discovered a cruel pleasure in playing the innocent. He could have pulled forward ten feet and done it again, but rolled around to the bottom of the drive where he could see both the approach and the overall layout of the doors. The drive was a gentle half circle, and one-way, so there was no checkpoint on this side. A truck going the wrong way could drive a load of explo-sives through the main doors without slowing.

"That would be useful," Lipschitz said on returning, "if we wanted to blow up the hospital, which we don't."

"We could use it as a diversion."

"To divert every soldier in the city here." He was sketching madly on a yellow pad, flipping pages, and didn't look up.

"I just thought I'd mention it."

"Thank you. Now can we be quiet for a few minutes? I need to remember this."

Eva thought it was a suicide mission. The prisoners were bait. Did Lipschitz see them? They might not even be there. And anyway, an operation like that would be strictly Irgun. They'd only used Lipschitz because he fit the role so perfectly.

131

Brand wanted to say they'd used him too, with all that that implied, but really, Asher had.

She might have been right, because instead of calling a meeting, Asher disappeared again.

With nothing to occupy his time, Brand planned his own rescue mission. It would happen late at night, a small operation, quiet, an inside job. Even then the hospital was full of workers. The orderlies could be paid off or blackmailed into leaving the right doors open. A few uniforms and name tags nicked from the laundry, a tray of syringes waiting at a nurses' station. Drug the guards' coffee and switch them with the prisoners, then take the prisoners out through the morgue to a waiting hearse. By morning they'd be in Tel Aviv with Begin.

Lipschitz had been drawing floor plans. Hallways and doctors' offices, the placement of elevators. As Brand hauled fares around town, he imagined himself creeping up a stairwell with a Sten. Behind him, silent as assassins, came Lipschitz and Fein and Yellin in black grease-paint, dressed like the Free French. Brand recognized the absurdity of the scene, something from a war movie. Neither did it escape him that in his daydreams he was Asher.

That Sunday he saw the blonde again, leaving a brunch fund-raiser for the Rockefeller Museum on the arm of an American air force colonel who helped her into the Daimler, tipped the valet and then took the wheel. He was strapping and blond, with the same well-fed aura of health and privilege. At a distance they might have been brother and sister. Could she be American? He'd figured her for a blue blood, an equestrian and adventuress, not some industrialist's daughter. He was two back in the queue and hemmed in by a line of mounted policemen so he couldn't follow them. On the steps, under a white muslin canopy erected to hold off the sun, the Rockefeller's benefactors waited in formal dress. Most had their own limousines, and by the time the valet waved for him, the Daimler was long gone.

By chance his passengers were Americans, an older couple Brand at first thought were doddering but soon realized had simply drunk too much. The valet helped the woman get her leg in and closed the door, then came around and gave Brand the address: the Palace Hotel, next to the American consulate. They didn't look like they were from the diplomatic corps.

"My God," the man said, "I thought we'd never get out of there."

"It's not my fault," the woman said. "Kitty said it would be fun."

"Fun," the man said, as if it were a curse.

"I liked those olives."

"They were good," he admitted. "And the little cheese things."

"The canapés. I still don't know what we're doing for dinner."

"I'm not hungry at all."

"You will be."

"Ask the driver."

"Yes, ma'am?" Jossi said.

"We're looking for someplace nice to eat, something local, not too expensive."

Pincus had taught him to send Americans to Fink's. They seemed pleased with the recommendation.

"Excuse me," Jossi said. "You are American?"

"Yes," the man said, interested.

"At the museum there was an American officer. We were betting, my friend and I. The lady he was with, I say she is a famous movie star. Blonde, like Veronica Lake."

"A movie star? I don't think so."

"He means the Rothschild girl," the woman said. "Tall, thin? She married the baron's son. You know, the one with the funny eye."

"She's not famous," the man said.

"Sorry," the woman said. "I hope you didn't bet much."

"Thank you," Jossi said.

It was no secret that the Rothschilds were connected to the Jewish Agency, and the Jewish Agency to the Haganah. The mystery was why she was with Asher. Maybe, as with Brand, he was her contact.

"She's very pretty," Eva said. "And Asher can be very charming."

Brand wanted to think Asher wouldn't let his feelings affect his judgment, but why should he, of all men, be exempt? If Brand were strictly following protocol, he wouldn't have said anything to Eva. He couldn't go to Asher either. From the first time he saw the blonde, he thought putting a name to her would ease his mind. Now he realized how great a complication she might be. The name was too large, like a secret too big to keep, and he was stuck with it.

Monday he waited at the King David, half expecting to see the Daimler. Spying behind his *Post*, he memorized the various approaches to the Secretariat, and later made a detailed sketch for Asher. It was like the hospital. While the south wing was heavily fortified, the main part of the hotel was wide open. Why bother with guards and barbed wire when you could walk through the front doors?

Tuesday they went to the Edison to see *Brief Encounter*. It played to a full house, and while Eva fell for the love story, Brand was distracted by the red exit signs on either side of the screen. At any moment someone could break through, shooting, and there was nowhere to run.

The next morning he took a team of Danish geologists from the train station to the potash works, driving across the blinding desert, then the steep descent to the Dead Sea, the hills of

Moab rising ash-gray out of the haze. It was a relief to be away from the city, and while the scientists had their meeting he walked the shore, skipping rocks, gulls winging overhead. On watch, those long nights, bound for Oran or Gibraltar, he'd lost himself in the vast, starry darkness, the tip of his cigarette a planet illuminating a strange hand that moved when he willed it. The waves here were tame, folding over themselves in the shallows without sound, and the scale less grand, but the sense that he was in the presence of the elemental was the same, and soothing. He wondered what night would be like.

Back in the city, he tried to recall the feeling, but it was gone, replaced by life and the Babel of traffic. On the Jaffa Road the cafés were packed. Barclays Bank had installed new blast-proof shutters over its windows. At every intersection he saw the possibility of disaster, and then, when it came, he wasn't ready.

As always, Eva was right. The hospital was a trap. An Irgun team tried to go in disguised as electricians. They never got past the checkpoint. The driver managed to turn around, but the truck hung up on a curb, and the gunner in the jeep blew out its tires. The driver died. Three others were in custody. The next day there were no gloating handbills, only the Mandate radio lauding the army. That night, in the searches that followed, they picked up Lipschitz.

# – 7 –

After a long evening of Carmel wine and cognac, Brand and Eva were dead asleep when there was a rapping at the door. It was past two, and reflexively he thought it was the police. They could go out the kitchen window and across the rooftops. His car was parked beside the Hurva.

"Stay here," she said, pulling on hcr robe. "It's probably just Mrs. Sokolov."

He kept still under the covers, listening as she unlocked the door. As she'd predicted, the voice was her landlady's, too soft for him to make out their conversation.

In a minute she returned, clicking on the bed-side lamp.

"You have to go."

"Now?"

"Now."

The police had Asher. To be safe they needed to break contact and go to ground for a while.

"I'm sorry," Eva said.

Stunned, Brand sat on the edge of the bed, pulling on his socks. Asher. It had to be a mistake. He couldn't imagine the cell without him. "What about Monday?"

137

"I'll call a taxi."

"Ask for Pincus. He's a friend."

He never suspected Mrs. Sokolov was one of them, and again he marveled at the reach of the underground. Who knew to call her?

He kept that in mind the next day as he drove, appraising the Canadian couple and the Uruguayan cleric and his secretary as if they might be spies. Taking the New Gate and sneaking through the linked courtyards of the Christian Quarter, he expected, any second, a gun to the back of his head. Instead, they tipped generously and blessed him. At home, his window open to the night, he waited for the low dieseling of an armored car and the rumble of jackboots on the stairs, the door cracking, but there was only Mrs. Ohanesian poking at Mozart, her budgie's irritating whistle.

When the Russians had first detained him, dragging him from his usual coffee shop, they wanted the names of everyone in the neighborhood who belonged to the army. Though it was common knowledge, Brand resisted, relenting only when they threatened his family. Knowing his own weakness, he ascribed it to Lipschitz—unfairly, perhaps. While Brand daydreamed of breaking into the hospital, Lipschitz had actually done it.

Asher. He still couldn't believe it.

Every instinct told him to flee. In an hour

he could be in Jaffa. His merchant seaman's papers were up-to-date. The docks worked round the clock. By morning he could be steaming for Lisbon or Port Said, leaving simple Jossi behind.

Without Eva, his days took the same shape. He woke, he drove, the perfect weather mocking him. Palm Sunday was almost upon them, and Pesach after that, the pageantry of Passion Week. The hotels were brimming with pilgrims. For lunch he ate falafel from his favorite vendor by the Damascus Gate, then a late dinner at the Alaska, finishing the night at his little table, sitting in the dark, nursing two fingers of scotch while the radio played. His cigar box was so stuffed with tips the lid wouldn't close. Now that he had money, he had no one to spend it on.

He worked the weekend, and on Monday gave Pincus a note for her—untraceable, he hoped. At noon he was in the Kidron Valley, taking an Argentinean family to the Gihon Spring, and couldn't swing by the King David. For Brand, the hardest part of her dates was when she came back to the car, babbling at him, happy to have his ear after being with a stranger. Now he thought he should be there to listen to her, as if he were shirking his duty.

The note Pincus returned with was unsigned as well, on plain paper. Her penmanship was surprisingly elegant, reminding him of his mother's: *I'm wearing your necklace. Be careful. I'll see you soon.*

"How is she?"

Pincus shrugged as if he had no opinion. "She looked good."

"Thank you for taking her." Brand tried to give him a pound, but Pincus fended it off. If he knew her as The Widow, he was too polite to say so, for which Brand was grateful. He didn't need to be told he was a fool.

He knew he should throw the note away or, better, burn it. He fit it in his cigar box, another treasure, and wondered what she'd done with his.

Tuesday was the eve of Pesach. By noon traffic had thinned as if the city were under curfew. Only the Arab buses were running. The streets of Mea Shearim and Mekor Baruch were deserted, the shops along the Jaffa Road closed. On Princess Mary Avenue a line of housewives waited on the sidewalk outside the one open grocer's, hoping he wouldn't run out of lamb shanks and horseradish.

Brand remembered his mother's endless preparations. She began cleaning weeks in advance, going through the house room by room, hunting down every crumb of chametz. When he and Giggi were little, she'd hide five pieces of bread for each of them so they could help. He took pride in finding his first until, one spring when he was six or seven, his mother came to him at bedtime and said it might be nice if he let his sister find hers first, and Brand understood that he'd been thoughtless. His joy poisoned, he turned dutiful, tagging after her with his own dust rag, rubbing at schmutz. When she finished a room, it was off-limits for eating. She did the kitchen last, on her hands and knees, digging in the cracks between the floorboards with tooth-picks, which his logical father—and Brand, his father's son—thought was going too far. The Udelsons were proper. His grandfather could perform the ceremony with the feather and the spoon and it would never be clean enough for his grandmother. The tears his mother shed making everything perfect for them. Even before they arrived, her failure was apparent. She didn't like their seder plate, which they'd received as a wedding present. There was the wine stain the dry cleaners could never get out of her good lace tablecloth, and now the kugel was ruined. She apologized, inconsolably angry, waiting for his grandmother to point out the obvious. "What a lovely table," his grandmother said. His grand-father wore the kittel, since his father wouldn't

It was a yearly ritual, the three generations gathered beneath the golden battlements of the lithograph, celebrating their freedom from Egypt and the mysterious bondage of family.

After such pains, to think it had all been swept away, burnt to cinders like the chametz, Brand himself the last remaining crumb.

Even Zion Square was empty, the students sent home for recess, Café Europa shuttered against the Shomrei Shabbat, fanatic Hasidim who tossed rocks through windows of businesses that didn't respect the Sabbath.

Baruch Hashem, there were always the tourists. Outside Herod's Gate, among the stooped water vendors and strutting pigeons, an American couple in matching sunglasses held a folding map between them, pointing in opposite directions. Brand swooped down on them like a hawk. It was their first day. Of course he knew where the Church of the Ascension was. He wouldn't recommend walking in this heat.

"Why is everything closed?" the husband asked when they were moving, leaning in close behind him.

*Why is this night different from all other nights?* For years, until Giggi could read, he was entrusted with the four questions, his grandfather comically drawing out the answers, making them wait before they could hide the afikoman and then find it later to claim their prize.

He adopted the couple, treating them to the best views from the Mount of Olives and all seven gates, selling them two rolls of film. When he dropped them at their hotel, the man shook his hand. If Jossi was ever in Boston, he should look them up. Brand imagined them showing him the town, the harbor lights and nightclubs, the dance-halls and neon boulevards he knew from the movies.

He'd never go. He was just lonely. It had only been four days since he'd spoken to her.

The Alaska would be closed, so he quit early and looped back to Princess Mary Avenue. The grocer's was still open. Brand parked and joined the line like a long-suffering husband sent on an errand. That there was wine left he counted a miracle.

In his room he prepared the feast. Thanks to the blackouts, he had candles. The one by his bed-side was just a nub, and he chose two new ones. Instead of his mother's sterling silver candle-sticks, used solely for this purpose, sharing the walnut hutch the rest of the year with her good crystal, he fit the candles into beer bottles and placed them on his bare table. It had been his mother's job to light the candles, then Giggi's, when she was old enough, and as he scratched a match against the side of the box and bent to touch the wavering flame to the wick, he saw his sister—ten or eleven, in her best Sabbath dress, her blond braids crowning her head like a milkmaid—circling their table, folding napkins and setting out the wineglasses, an extra goblet in the middle for Elijah. Though he was only one tonight, Brand did the same, as if he were drinking with the prophet.

After sundown, he took the pillow from his bed and tucked it behind him on his chair so he could recline as he told the story.

Like his grandfather, he blessed the wine. As a child he hadn't listened, and his Kiddush was makeshift. After a taste of sweetness, he had to walk down the hall to the bathroom to wash his hands, then came back and started on the seder plate. Here was the parsley dipped in salt water to remember the tears of the people, the egg and the lamb shank, the bitter herbs. He broke the middle matzoh and asked himself the four questions, for years his only real Hebrew, the sacred language diligently memorized, indelible yet rote, never fully taken to heart. Like his father, bored by the pomp and pace of the ceremony, he was a skeptic, leery of any outward show, except even then, in his rational lack of faith, he felt guilty. Now he could see he wasn't the wicked child, as he'd sometimes thought, or as he suspected later, the simple one, but, like his father, the one who didn't know how to ask. Proud Brand. Why did he think he knew more than God?

He dipped a finger in his wine and spilled a drop on the table for each of the ten plagues. As children they thrilled at the rain of blood, he frogs and lice and flies. This was their favorite part, God's messy retribution on their persecutors, even as Grandfather Udelson reminded them that no one should take pleasure in the sufferings of God's creatures. The lesson seemed even truer now, after the camps, as did the idea that in every generation each of them needed to realize they'd been delivered from Egypt, and for the first time, sitting there in the shifting candlelight, recalling all he'd lost, Brand understood there was a reason he'd been spared.

The meal itself wasn't worthy of his mother, but he ate the matzoh ball soup and roast chicken and fruit compote gratefully, wishing Eva were there to share it with him. He thought of Asher and Lipschitz in detention, and their families at home. In the camps, when there was no food, the devout celebrated with the word. Brand in his disillusion abstained, an evasion he regretted now. He wished he were a better Jew. This was a start.

For Giggi he'd hidden the afikoman behind his radio. At home, for finding it, their grandfather gave them each a shiny silver five-lats coin which his mother insisted they put in the bank. Now Brand didn't need a prize. He could recall only a few lines of the psalms, and said their everyday grace, still intact after all these years. He filled Elijah's cup and opened the door for him, then sat back down as if to wait.

"Next year in Jerusalem," Brand said, and drank to the dead and to the future.

A cuckoo had built a nest in the cemetery. As if in rebuttal, it started up its monotonous call. Outside his window, beyond the darkened crypts and the Church of the Dormition, the wall by the Zion Gate glowed a lurid honey-gold in the floodlights. With the holiday, the British were on high alert. Eva had made it clear they should have no contact, yet, as if he'd had a vision, Brand wanted to go and tell her what had happened. This was what he'd come to Jerusalem to find, a new purpose, and as he washed his dishes in the bathroom sink, moved by his revelation, he thought recklessly of proposing to her.

By morning his wits had returned. She was no believer, and might be angry with him for asking too much of her. He'd confused religion and emotion, the universal and the personal. With no one to confide in, the excitement he'd felt seemed private and suspect, the product of alcohol, nostalgia and loneliness—except he *had* been delivered out of this last Egypt, along with a million and a half others, and the fact that he was here, now, among thousands of them, wasn't luck or chance but history. He was free. What he did now was up to him, so while he didn't run out and join the nearest temple, he felt renewed, and when, Maundy Thursday, Fein called to say their young friend was out of the hospital, Brand saw it as a sign.

"He's not well enough to visit," Fein said. "He needs rest."

"Is it all right if I give him a call?"

"I'd wait. He may be contagious."

"I'm glad he's feeling better."

"So are we," Fein said.

He thought of sending Pincus to her flat with a message, but knew he was being stupid. When had he become so impatient? For years all he'd done was wait.

It was Passion Week, and the Old City was choked with processions. Gentiles of every sect traced Christ's steps along the Via Dolorosa, stopping at the numbered Stations of the Cross to take pictures of the reenactors and buy mementos from the Moslem shopkeepers. Brand made a killing selling film and running people up the Mount of Olives. Time moved faster when he was busy, and like an actual cabbie he was grateful for the crowds.

Easter Sunday the draw was the Church of the Holy Sepulchre. He was second in the queue at the Jaffa Gate when he noticed an Arab at the head of the line give his spot to the couple behind him so he could ride with Brand. He was short and pale, in a black kaftan and keffiyeh, ducking behind the couple as if to hide. Among the pilgrims clutching olivewood crosses and the tourists draped with cameras he was conspicuous, and as soon as Brand pulled up and saw the glasses and piggy cheeks he knew who was beneath this hapless disguise.

Brand flashed on driving right past him, but Lipschitz grabbed the door handle and let himself in.

"Jossi, it wasn't me, you've got to believe me. They all think it was me, but it wasn't."

"I don't know what they think."

"Someone broke into my flat while I was away. No one will talk to me."

"We're not supposed to be talking to anyone."

"I swear I didn't say anything. You know me, I wouldn't do that."

"I know you wouldn't," Brand said to calm him down. "Where do you want to go?"

"Eva's."

"We can't go to Eva's."

"Your place."

"You know I can't do that." Lipschitz probably had a sketch of it showing all the exits.

"I can't go back to my flat. They're watching it."

They were probably watching them now, Brand thought. "Do you want me to take you to the station?"

"That won't help. Tell Gideon I didn't say anything."

"When would I talk to Gideon?"

"Tell Eva."

He couldn't lie, and after everything, he couldn't say no. "I'll try."

"Thank you, Jossi. I knew you'd help me. You saved me before."

"It may take a while. We're not supposed to be talking to anyone right now."

"I'm sorry, I didn't know what else to do."

"Where do you want to go?"

They were cruising along Sultan Suleiman Street in the shadow of the wall. Lipschitz twisted round to watch the cars following them as if they were being tailed. Across from the Damascus Gate was the Arab bus station. In their numbered stalls, under a shady overhang, a dozen coaches waited to take him to Nablus and Beersheba and Jericho.

"Want me to drop you at the station?"

"No. Turn here."

They headed for the western suburbs. Instead of shooting straight out the Jaffa Road, he had Brand detour north through the Russian Compound, then left on the Street of the Prophets, cutting up to Mea Shearim until the traffic behind them had dwindled. He checked over his shoulder before telling Brand where to turn next. As Brand had guessed when they were casing the substation, Lipschitz was from the teeming apartment blocks of Zikhron Moshe. Instead of taking a room in an obscure corner of the city, he was hoping to disappear into the familiar alleys and boarding-houses of this far-flung outpost of Kraków.

Brand let him off outside a bookbinder's with the slate of the Workers' Party decorating its window.

"Be careful," Brand said.

"Tell them."

"I will."

"Thank you. You be careful too."

Brand gave him a last wave, and once he was in traffic and free of him, banged the steering wheel with the heel of his hand. "Damn it."

Contagious, Fein said. As Brand would be if anyone found out. How was he supposed to tell Eva, and who was she supposed to convince?

*You saved me before.* Brand cringed, remembering. He hadn't saved him, it was just a splinter. He'd never saved anybody.

His hope was that Asher would be released, relieving him of the responsibility, but tomorrow was Monday. At his table, by lamplight, he toiled over his note to Eva. Below, Mrs. Ohanesian stumbled through a Chopin étude, making him start again. He was a poor spy. He didn't know any secret codes, and every metaphor seemed obvious and incriminating.

*Our young friend is out of the hospital but feeling lonely. Please let everyone know he's no longer contagious. He's had laryngitis for two weeks and would love to talk to someone.*

She wrote back: *The doctors said no visitors for a reason. The most important thing for him now is rest.*

Brand thought her advice wise, but with no way to tell Lipschitz, felt he hadn't fully discharged his duty. Every time he queued up at the Jaffa Gate, he expected to see the pantomime Arab standing in line. In his flat, when the phone rang, he cocked his head, froze until Mrs. Ohanesian closed her door again. Like Lipschitz, he was turning squirrelly on his own.

Two days later, the radio broke the silence. While he was sleeping, an Irgun team masquerading as policemen bringing in a busload of Arab detainces had raided a detention camp in Ramat Gan, liberating a dozen prisoners and the contents of the armory. "This is the voice of Fighting Zion," the announcer heroically signed off, and though he had no evidence, Brand was convinced Asher was one of them.

Lipschitz must have figured Asher had escaped, because that morning when Brand called in from the Jaffa Gate, Greta had a pickup for a Mr. Ge'ula in Zikhron Moshe. Mr. Hope. He thought it was unfair of Lipschitz, and on the way out, checking his mirrors to make sure no one was following him, Brand bit his cheek, trying to find the right words to tell him this had to stop.

The address was a basement flat in the rear of a cement apartment block, the kind of dingy hiding place Brand himself would choose. The back door was riveted steel, the windows louvered slits at ground level to let some light in, and as he pulled the Peugeot abreast of the stairwell, he noticed the pair on the left was boarded over. He expected the place was fortified, wired with Asher's favorite booby-traps, and rather than risk tripping one, he didn't get out, just honked twice, lightly. Lipschitz could come to him.

He honked again, longer.

When there was no answer, like a bit player in a movie, he called, "Taxi! Taxi for Mr. Ge'ula!"

He didn't turn the car off, left the driver's side open as he approached the entrance. The cement of the stairwell was cracked. At the bottom a mat of trash and wet leaves had gathered in one corner. Brand examined the lock. Years of keys had left scratches in the brass. It was impossible to tell if it was rigged. By twisting the knob, he might be wrapping a half-inch of piano wire around the other side, pulling the pin on a homemade grenade, the blast unleashing a handyman's blend of shrapnel—fence staples and roofing nails and wood screws.

He knocked.

"Mr. Ge'ula."

He knocked harder.

He scanned the backs of the other tenements

to see if right now Lipschitz was watching him. That was the problem with going out on your own. You had only one set of eyes.

He thumped the door with a fist and called for him again, then dropped his hand to the knob and, averting his face, turned it gently, listening for a click.

The door opened.

A dank concrete hallway, dimly lit and smelling of dead mice, ran the length of the basement. The number Greta had given him matched the first flat on the left—the one with the boarded-up windows. He knocked, expecting nothing, and was surprised to hear from the other side a faint scratching, like a cat asking to be let out.

"Taxi," Brand said.

The scratching stopped, making him stoop to see if he could pick it up again.

It might just be mice.

"Mr. Ge'ula."

He dropped to one knee and pressed an ear to the door like a safecracker. Nothing, but now a second smell reached him, familiar yet unwelcome, and he recalled the scene in Eva's bright bedroom and, later, kneeling in the driveway, scrubbing his backseat.

The door, for all his precautions, was unlocked. It opened a few inches, then abruptly stuck, caught on Lipschitz's hand like a doorstop.

He was facedown, reaching for the door as if

to answer it. A dark smear stretched across the linoleum behind him. He must have crawled.

His hand was still warm. Brand moved it and sidled through. He turned Lipschitz over. His throat was cut, his shirt soaked. He was missing his glasses and his face was swollen, his eyes rolled back, showing the whites. Brand wanted to ask who'd done this to him, but saw it was useless.

At second glance, he knew who it was. As a message, they'd cut out his tongue.

Brand didn't stick around to find it.

# – 8 –

With the dry season came the heat, and the khamsin, whipping in from across the desert, topping the walls, chasing through the alleys of the four quarters, sending whirlwinds skirling down the lanes of the suburbs. The sky was gray and freighted with dust, the cypresses rustling in advance of a storm that built all day, promising relief, yet never arrived. At night the air was suffocating, and it was impossible to sleep. In his skivvies Brand sat at his window, smoking black market Gitanes, looking down on the huddled domes of the Old City. The cuckoo sent up its two-toned call like a broken clock.

Asher was in hiding, probably in Tel Aviv, pulling strings like Begin. Victor was their contact now, Gideon their commander. The killing of Lipschitz was official, a necessary security measure, a proclamation as blatant as the memorial handbills pasted about town, a plain black border containing his alias, at once a tribute and a warning. The *Post* identified him as Yaakov Ben Mazar, a watchmaker's apprentice and lifelong member of Congregation B'nai Avraham of Zikhron Moshe. He would always be Lipschitz, squinting behind his glasses.

Eva tried to defend the murder to Brand, as if he were an innocent. She didn't like it either, especially the execution, but they couldn't take the chance. Lipschitz had cracked and given up Asher, compromising all of them.

She knew that for a fact?

They knew it, and she believed them. They had people inside the CID.

What if they were wrong? Brand asked.

If they were wrong, they'd be forgiven.

So killing was no longer a sin?

Not in the cause of freedom. He was being impossible. He wanted a revolution without bloodshed.

No, he wanted a revolution that was just.

Just. What did they do with informers in Latvia? In the camps?

Brand was unconvinced. Lipschitz visited him nightly, begging him to plead his case. *Jossi, it wasn't me.* To his eternal shame, Brand hedged, condemning him. That wasn't what happened, the conscious Brand argued, but as the days passed, he grew to understand he'd betrayed him by his silence, as he'd betrayed Koppelman and Katya and everyone he loved. He had the selfish habit of saving his own life.

He needed to rely on it now. As Lipschitz's go-between, he was suspect. At the garage, while Pincus was chatty as ever, Scheib was quiet, and Brand wondered how much they knew. Victor didn't have a role for him in their next operation, which didn't make sense. He was the only one with a car. Following protocol, while the rest of the cell met at the high school, Brand waited outside in the Peugeot. On the drive home, Fein and Yellin sat in back. Though he hadn't seen them in weeks, they had nothing to say. No one spoke of Lipschitz, as if he'd never been their friend.

"Of course no one knows what to say," Eva said. "We're in shock."

She didn't tell him what the job was. He understood. Because she was with him, she was suspect. If anything went wrong, she'd take the blame. From the minute he recognized Lipschitz beneath his disguise, that was exactly what Brand was afraid of. There was no one he could appeal to, no way to explain. So the murder had worked. From then on, they all kept their mouths shut.

He thought the operation might take place on Lag B'Omer and involve a fire around sundown, in accordance with the story. There were oil refineries and pipelines everywhere, stores of kerosene. The British had the same idea, and tightened security as the day neared. At five they called curfew and closed the gates of the Old City, prompting a riot among the younger Hasidim they countered with mounted police. The post office that burned in Mahane Yehuda was the spontaneous act of a mob, though the next day the *Post* gleefully pointed out the symbolism.

The train station. The YMCA. It was impossible not to speculate. His passengers parroted the same rumors that had been circulating for months.

The British held off sentencing the Sarafand prisoners, afraid it might trigger riots. The khamsin was blowing, and the whole country was restless. In Jaffa and Tel Aviv the telephone workers went on strike, Jews and Arabs both. No one blamed them. During the war prices had skyrocketed while wages stayed the same. The civil servants walked out in sympathy, followed by the railway workers and longshore-men. When the shipping lines tried to bring in strikebreakers, there were bloody skirmishes on the docks.

Brand's American fares worried about the communists' influence.

"People just want to eat," Jossi reassured them.

Monday he was back driving Eva to the King David, imagining the man balling his socks and shutting the closet door. Their affair had gone on too long for simple blackmail. She had to be gathering information on the Secretariat, maybe on the floor plan, which offices belonged to what branch of the Mandate. The elevator was a natural place for an assassination. He could walk right in as if he were looking for her, press the button and watch the arrow slowly sweep through the numbers, though the lobby was probably seeded with plainclothesmen. Once in the elevator, he'd choose the preordained floor, then draw his gun, aiming for the center of the doors at chest level—or eye level, since the high commissioner was tall. Neither of them would survive, but there would be that exhilarating descent, knowing he'd struck a blow for his people. The next day his name would be on light poles and kiosks up and down the Jaffa Road.

Daydreaming Brand, waiting for her, as always. She was late. He tried not to let it bother him. He pretended to read the paper, watching the front doors and the drive behind him in the mirror. He hadn't seen the Daimler since the museum, but kept an eye on the new arrivals. He wondered if the heiress was with Asher in Tel Aviv, the two of them shacked up in a sea-side tourist court like Bonnie and Clyde. He wondered if she knew about Lipschitz and his tongue.

When Eva finally came out, she was with Edouard from the Kilimanjaro, laughing at some joke, a hand on his arm. To Brand it seemed dangerous, the two of them meeting in public. Even off-duty, in the midday sun, Edouard wore a morning coat. She kissed him on both cheeks and he set off down the drive toward the guard-house.

"Does he want a ride?" Brand asked.

"He's not going that far."

She was struggling with the catch of the pendant, her head bent, her chin tucked to her chest. He wanted to ask what they were laughing about—how could she after having just been with her Englishman?—but knew it would end badly. With a professional patience, he waited for an explanation.

"Really, don't be jealous. He was just having his hair cut."

"Here?"

"They're very good, but very expensive. It's impossible to get an appointment. Not for Edouard, of course. He knows everyone. I wish you liked him more."

"I like him enough, I just don't know him very well."

"He's a darling, that's all you need to know about him."

They left the hotel grounds and turned up the broad boulevard of Julian's Way, crossing Abraham Lincoln Street. Again, like a teacher, he waited.

"We had a drink, just one. I think I've earned one drink."

"You have." That explained the laughter, and the glibness. He doubted it was just one.

She had a double brandy at her flat, and poured herself another before he said he had to get back.

"Stay with me," she said. "Take the day off."

"I wish I could."

"I hate when you're like this."

"Like what?"

"Mad at me. Do you want me to tell you what it is? Is that what you want?"

"No."

"It's where they fix the trains." The railyards in Lydda. His first thought was that it was too far, they had to pass too many checkpoints.

"I said I didn't want to know."

"I told them you should drive. They said they already had someone."

"Stop it."

"It's not my fault. You're the one who wanted me to tell them."

It was true. He'd put her in the same position Lipschitz had put him. "I know it isn't."

"Then why do you make me feel like it is?"

"If it's anyone's fault, it's mine. I didn't know."

"What did you think was going to happen?"

"I didn't think they'd kill him."

"That's your problem—you don't think. You shouldn't have given your friend those notes."

"Pincus."

"It's not his fault," she said. "He was just doing what he's supposed to."

Pincus, Greta. He wondered when the call from Lipschitz had come in. They'd given the killer the address and a head start. That was why there were no booby-traps. Lipschitz thought it was him at the door.

"He trusted me."

"It would have happened anyway," Eva said. "Now you have people worrying about you."

"And you."

"And me. So stop wallowing and start thinking. You don't want people worrying about you."

He agreed, he needed to be smarter. Then why, he wondered afterward, did she tell him about the job? He suspected it was a test. At the garage he played dumb, palling around with Pincus and Scheib as if nothing had happened. As he drove, he planned the operation like a tactician. A night raid on the repair sheds, their faces blackened with greasepaint. Unlike the tracks, the engines were irreplaceable, new diesels shipped from England. Every evening she was unavailable, he waited for the radio to confirm it, and then, one morning the week after Shavuot, as he was delivering a Lebanese couple to the Pool of Bethesda, the Voice of Fighting Zion celebrated another glorious victory at Lydda Junction. Freedom fighters had blown up a locomotive and burned a dozen coaches belonging to the occupa-tion. The announcer said nothing about the roundhouse or the fuel depot, nothing about the repair sheds themselves. Brand expected more damage.

"It was a mess," Eva said. "Two of the charges didn't go off, and one barely did anything. We needed you and Asher."

And Lipschitz, he thought.

He couldn't ask who else had gone along, and listened to find out. Fein, Yellin, Victor—all that was left of the cell. The driver's name was Thierry. Another Frenchman. Again, Brand wondered if her drink with Edouard had been a coincidence.

"Victor had us pull back when the charges didn't go off. Asher would have stayed and fixed them."

"Asher's would have gone off." So, no Gideon. Why was he surprised?

"I wish you'd have been there."

"Me too."

He thought he shouldn't be so pleased the action was a failure. Though it proved nothing, he counted their misfortune toward his case for reinstatement. Asher had chosen him for the substation and praised him after the train. What had changed?

The Lydda raid prompted the usual curfews and searches, leading to the usual random arrests. Despite the radio's claims, it meant little strategically, except that the revolution had become a war of gestures. The British were through being humiliated. A few days later, a military court found the Sarafand prisoners guilty and sentenced them to death. The women received ten years each. In retaliation, a gunman in the back of a speeding cab sprayed a group of soldiers patrolling Julian's Way, killing two. Brand cursed the news, knowing it would make things harder for him.

That night, minutes after he'd come back from the Alaska, Mrs. Ohanesian's phone rang. It was Fein, earning Brand the fisheye.

"This is Mr. Grossman. My train comes in at eight fifteen and I need a ride."

"Certainly, sir."

There was no eight fifteen, and no Grossman, only Fein himself waiting at the station, dressed in black, as if for a funeral, carrying a familiar valise. He kept it balanced across his knees in the backseat.

"Where are we going?" Brand asked.

Fein had him head north toward the city, then turn into the grid of Yemin Moshe, long, low stucco apartment blocks gliding by on both sides. The streetlights were out, and the moon cast shadows over the road. In the gray light, as the same buildings repeated, regular as barracks, it struck Brand that the neighborhood was laid out like the camps.

"Up here," Fein said, pointing to a corner block. "Flash your lights."

As they rolled to a stop, the front door of a villa opened and three figures scurried across the yard, hunched as if under fire. Fein shifted noisily to make room. Brand stretched for the passenger door and let in Gideon, dressed, like Fein, entirely in black. In back, Victor and Yellin wore the same uniform. Brand thought they could have told him.

The car was full. They weren't taking Eva, and he understood the operation was yet another test. While he resented the implication, he was grateful for the chance to prove himself again. Wasn't that all Lipschitz had wanted?

"We need to go east," Gideon said.

This time of night, five men in a taxi would never get through a checkpoint. Brand avoided the Old City, detouring through the American Colony and out the Jericho Road. While they were busy evading patrols, the moon outraced them, hanging bright as a spotlight above the desert. In its pale glare, every shadow might be hiding a jeep. Beside him, in Gideon's lap, a nickel-plated pistol glinted. Brand wished he had his. He couldn't ask where they were going. He had half a tank of gas, and scourged himself for not filling up after work. It didn't matter that they'd given him no warning. He was a soldier. From now on he needed to be prepared. As the Peugeot ate up the miles, no one spoke. He thought they should be monitoring the radio, but drove in silence, his eyes on the road, all the while figuring out his best play, as if he were their hostage.

They came down from Bethany into the Jordan Valley, dipping below sea level, the descent making his ears pop. It was Arab territory, the terraced hills dotted with whitewashed villages. He'd driven the road dozens of times, though never at night, for fear of bandits. The tourists had to see the tomb of Lazarus and the walls of Jericho and finally the River Jordan, wading its brackish shallows with their cuffs rolled up, filling vials to take home, as if the slimy water were a curative. Ahead on their right stood the Inn of the Good Samaritan, who'd helped the man fallen in with thieves. On the hilltop above it loomed the ruins of Qa'alat ed-Dum— the Castle of Blood, a trap for weary travelers and highwaymen alike.

"Take the old road," Gideon said.

It would be harder on the car, plus they'd look suspicious, Brand wanted to protest, but slowed and eased the front wheels down over the lip of the pavement onto the rocky hardpan, the suspension juddering. The Romans had built the road, and no one had fixed it since. Ditches ran on both sides. He kept to the crown, deeply incised by the spring rains. Every so often the nose of the car dropped into a trough, pitching them forward. Gideon braced himself against the dash. In back Fein clutched the valise to his lap. Brand supposed that after the Lydda fiasco, Asher had packed the charges himself. Brand under-stood. You could trust others only so far.

He thought the target would be in Jericho, a local armory or provincial court, but they kept going, skirting the town limits, angling north along the border across the salt flats, following a road impassable any other season. Behind him Yellin coughed as if he'd swallowed something wrong. Victor thumped his back and Fein laughed.

"I'm all right," Yellin said. "Stop."

"Enough," Gideon said.

There were no trains out here, no British installations, only the sluggish river on their right, the banks lined with thirsty willows and tamarisks. They weren't far from the Franciscan chapel commemorating John's baptism of Jesus, always good for a few pictures. Dead south of them, on the main road, the Allenby Bridge was modern, guarded by a manned blockhouse, the span marking the gateway to Trans-Jordan. Here, where the river was a trickle, there was only an ancient stone arch used by goatherds whose loyalties were tribal. In the morning they drove their goats into Palestine, and in the evening drove them back again without visa.

"Slow down," Gideon said, checking his watch, confirming Brand's guess.

The bridge might have had a troll living beneath it. Over the centuries, generations of masons had slapped mortar over the stones haphazardly, giving the walls the appearance of lumpy stucco. Brand clenched his jaw and was glad for the darkness. For this they risked their lives?

"Keep it running," Gideon said, getting out.

The rest followed, leaving their doors open to the cool night air.

Brand dimmed his lights. The engine chugged, the low idle providing cover for anyone who might be sneaking up on him. It was just nerves. They were alone out here—no patrols, no bandits lurking in the shadows, nothing but hoofprints and dung, the sewer-like stink of the river. By electric torchlight, Fein set the valise on the ground and divvied up the charges. Gideon and Victor crossed to the east bank. Fein and Yellin ducked under the near side. For a moment Brand couldn't see any of them, and then Gideon and Victor came loping back over the bridge, their faces floating ghostly in the darkness. Fein and Yellin returned and took their places again, Fein resting the valise on his knees.

"Everything good?" Gideon asked.

"Everything's good," Fein said.

"Okay," Gideon told Brand, and he hit the lights and started off.

It was faster coming back. Now that he knew

the road, he could push the car harder. A moth thumped the windshield, leaving a powdery smudge.

"We've got lots of time," Gideon said, and Brand slowed. *We.* Had he passed the test? But he'd done nothing.

Against instinct, he held back, rocking along, anticipating the blast in his rearview mirror. The British would call curfew and throw up road-blocks. He'd have to drop everyone in the desert and take his chances. Maybe the test was just being there, one of them again. He didn't have to be a hero. He was a driver. He drove.

They went on across the salt plain, retracing their own tracks, sneaking past sleepy Jericho. Asher must have used a timer. As with the substation, Brand never heard the charges go off. Sooner than expected they reached the main road and turned for Jerusalem, cruising over the smooth asphalt, racing the moon. For miles the highway was empty, the first set of headlights a shock, as if they'd been caught—a semi headed for the potash works. Beside him, Gideon slipped his gun into his pocket.

They didn't go back to Yemin Moshe. Gideon had him drop him and Victor off in Sheikh Jarrah, an Arab neighborhood north of the city that Brand visited only to fill up on cheap gas. Fein and Yellin he let off in Rehavia, not far from the high school.

"Long live Eretz Israel," they said.

"Long live Eretz Israel."

Alone again, he switched on the radio, hoping to hear news from Jericho, and wasn't surprised there was nothing. Asher himself had taught him. A clock could be set for twelve hours.

When he pulled in the drive, Mrs. Ohanesian's lights were off. His flat was an oven, and he stayed up late, sitting at his window, sipping, going over his strange night—driving through the moonlit desert with Gideon to blow up a goat bridge. In the morning it had the feeling of a dream, until the Voice of Fighting Zion proclaimed a great victory. In a coordinated strike, fighters had destroyed a dozen bridges on the borders of their Arab neighbors, including the main rail link to Syria. Eleven members of the Stern Gang had given their lives. As with the train, Brand realized the importance of their mission only after the fact. Now he was proud, when, waiting for them to set the charges, he'd been chary, unsure why they were there, and again he reproached himself for being so cautious, as if he might change his nature.

That afternoon in Tel Aviv, the Irgun stormed a British officers' club, absconding with five hostages. The army called curfew and cordoned off the city.

Eva said she didn't know anything about the bridge job.

"That's good," she said. "Everyone's being careful."

"I guess," Brand said. "I like to know what I'm doing."

"It's nice that you get to choose. Not like the rest of us."

"All I'm asking for is a little warning."

"I don't think you're in a position to ask for anything."

"Don't I know it." Neither are you, he might have said, thanks to him.

He stayed the night, listening to her sleep, the combined heat of them making him sweat where he draped an arm over her. He'd become used to Katya visiting him here, in her rival's bed, looked forward to it like a favorite dream. Now when she didn't come, he had to conjure her from memory, a trick that grew harder and harder, contaminated as it was by his visions of Crow Forest, the naked dead piled like so many hog carcasses. He considered it a failure on his part that he could barely hear her voice anymore, as if he were purposely forgetting her.

In the morning the sheets smelled of perfume and he didn't want to leave. In her housecoat, Eva made him breakfast, teasing that she was going back to sleep. The Mandate radio said the terrorists had condemned the kidnapped men to death.

"Naturally," Brand said.

"They have to know we're serious."

"I think they know by now."

"They hang our people for less."

On that point he couldn't argue, and yet, likely because he'd been a prisoner, he refused to accept execution as a weapon. But that was war, wasn't it, a contest of executions? In this case he expected the threat was defensive. "I think we're trying to set up a trade."

"They have to know we'll go through with it."

"Of course." Because even in their depleted cell, the will was there. If not Asher, then Gideon or Victor or whoever killed Lipschitz. Again, though he knew better, he had trouble imagining a Jew without mercy. Softhearted Brand, the eternal greenhorn. Why did he think his people, of all God's tribes, were exempt?

While Tel Aviv was shut down, in Jerusalem traffic moved freely. Around the Old City the British stood watch, Airborne troops massed at checkpoints as if waiting for a signal. In the late afternoon it came, and they barricaded the gates with barbed wire and armored cars. News ricocheted through the queue. Another officer had been kidnapped, taken in broad daylight from the new city center, chloroformed and shoved in a taxi, a Panama hat stuck on his head. Immediately Brand thought of Pincus, an easy leap he later had to retract. The cab had been stolen, found abandoned in the Bukharan Quarter. The radio identified the victim as a Major H. P. Chadwick, married, the father of two. Before the evening call to prayer, the Irgun broadcast his death sentence.

With the Old City and the western suburbs cut off, Brand retreated to the Damascus Gate, picking up fares at the bus station, fitting their luggage in the trunk. The buses from Nablus and Ramallah and Jericho were running, but the British were stopping everything from the west. Arabs didn't tip, and once night had fallen, the neighborhoods north of the city were dangerous. After his dinner of falafel, he used the call box to check in with Greta. He had a pickup in Sheikh Jarrah, a Mr. Grossman.

"Yes," Brand said. "I know him."

It wasn't Fein, as he'd expected, but Victor, waiting on the cobbled drive of a gated villa.

"Get out of the car," the Frenchman said.

"Why?" Brand asked, but there was no sense protesting.

"Turn around."

Brand stood still as a man being fitted for a suit as Victor tied a blindfold over his eyes, then covered his head with a bag-like hood.

"Duck," Victor said, palming Brand's skull, and folded him into the backseat.

Sightless, suffocating inside the musty hood, Brand braced himself as they rumbled down the drive and swung right. To confuse him, Victor turned into the side streets, executing a series of rights and lefts, making Brand grab the seat back. He wished he knew the area better, though soon enough they straightened out, cruising over a smooth road, speeding up, the engine laboring before Victor finally shifted to third. Brand counted the seconds as if he might re-create the directions later. The farther they went without slowing, the more convinced he was they were going north on the Nablus Road, into the desert. He was even more certain when they braked and pulled off onto the rocky shoulder. They sat like that for a minute, and then Brand heard a second engine approaching, and the telltale crunch of another car pulling in behind them, and people getting out.

The door beside Brand opened, letting in the night air. Someone took his elbow and pulled him out, bumping his head, instantly giving him a headache. He bent at the waist to keep his feet as they marched him to the other car. Even through the hood, the interior stank of clove oil, a common deodorizer around the garage, and again he thought of Pincus. The driver said nothing, just drove. Behind them Brand could hear the Peugeot, its familiar purr a comfort.

They were taking him to see Asher, he figured, or maybe the Old Man himself, flushed from Tel Aviv by the crackdown. He understood the precautions but not why he alone had been

174

summoned, unless it had something to do with Lipschitz. Had Eva pleaded his case, as Brand asked, or turned him in? Her loyalty was unswerving, sealed with blood, while Brand's was still unproven. This might be another test, or was that done with? They might never take the hood off, drive him into the desert and leave him there, naked, a bullet behind one ear, the Peugeot fated to be painted again, loaned to another Jossi. They'd want a public place, to send a message. But they could have done that any time. Why, the wise child in him asked, was this night different from all other nights?

They had to be almost to Ramallah. On and on they droned, making him doubt his instincts. When they veered onto another paved road without braking, he admitted he was lost and surrendered to the noise and the darkness.

Miles later, when they finally stopped, he kept quiet, hoping to identify the men's voices as they pulled him out, but no one spoke. This time he was careful of his head. They led him away like a prisoner, one at each elbow. He swore one was wearing perfume—or, no, cologne. Maybe Edouard or Thierry, their new driver.

"Step up," Victor, on his right, said.

A door opened, emitting a whiff of onions cooking in oil and the babbling of a radio. Inside, the house was hot, making him sweat. They crossed what he imagined was a long room—

though it might have been two—and stopped. A door opened, and Victor took Brand's wrist and placed his hand on a banister.

"Step down," he said, counting as they went. ". . . eleven, twelve."

The basement was cooler, and humid, with a hint of mold. They turned left, paused for a door, crossed a room and paused again.

"Duck," Victor said, and Brand did.

The door closed behind them, a metal latch falling to with a clank, recalling his grand-mother's root cellar, though the floor here was wooden. Close by, a chair scraped the boards, bumping the back of his knees. Victor pressed on his shoulder, and once Brand had sat down, pulled off the hood. Out of reflex, Brand grabbed at the blindfold.

The light made him blink. A bare bulb hung above a cheap sheet-metal desk. Across from him sat Asher, except his hair was jet-black rather than gray, most strikingly his eyebrows. His cheeks, as in Brand's vision of his grand-mother, were dirty, stained the brown of shoe polish, as if he were trying to pass for a Yemeni. Only as Brand's eyes grew used to the light did he see the coloring wasn't a disguise but from bruising, the skin turned the caramel of apples gone bad. Asher's face was swollen, his left eye shut, his forehead, nose and chin livid with purple scabs. His hands were splinted, bandaged into mitts.

"It looks worse than it is." He even sounded different, his lips barely moving, and Brand saw his jaw was wired shut. "Sorry about the extra security measures. Obviously we have a problem."

"I understand."

"Do you?" Asher studied him as if he were guarding a secret. Victor stood behind him, a silent bodyguard.

"I do," Brand said. So it was about Lipschitz. About him.

Asher patted a mitt against the table and looked to the ceiling, as if chasing a stray thought. "Do you know a woman named Emilie de Rothschild?"

Brand feared the surprise on his face was a give-away. "I don't know her, but I've heard of her."

"You've seen her."

"I've seen her."

"She seems to think you're following her. Why would she think that?"

"I don't know," Brand said.

"You haven't been following her."

"I did once, to see who she was."

"To see who she was." With effort, Asher twisted to look at Victor. "And who is she?"

"One of the Rothschilds."

"What would you say if I told you she's my wife?"

Now Brand tried to act surprised.

"She's not," Asher said, "but I have a responsibility to her and to her family that's just as great. The way I'm responsible to you and Eva and Victor. The way Lipschitz was supposed to be responsible to all of us." He pointed to his face, nodding as if it were proof. "Do you understand?"

"Yes."

"Leave her alone. She attracts enough attention as it is. Now, how much do you know about what Eva's doing at the King David?"

"Not a lot."

"Be specific, please."

The only thing Brand left out was the part about the socks and the closet.

"That's good. You never want to know more than you need to. Eva doesn't need to know we've talked, is that clear?"

"Yes." Though it wasn't at all.

"I have a job for you. No one can know about it. Will you do it for me?"

"Yes."

"Thank you." He reached a mitt across the table for Brand to take. Each finger was taped to a tongue depressor. It felt like a paddle. "Go with Victor."

As he rose, Asher remained seated, and Brand suspected he couldn't stand. What else had they done to him? In the darkness against the wall rested a cot, in the corner a tin pail. He was living down here like a prisoner, like Lipschitz in his booby-trapped flat.

The job was a delivery. Brand didn't have to see the bulky sack swinging between Victor and Gideon as they lugged it across the courtyard and lowered it into his trunk to know it was Major Chadwick. The Peugeot was pointed toward a high iron gate, beyond which stretched the lightless desert. Though the knowledge provided only a grim satisfaction, he'd been right about the Nablus Road. Against all logic he was taking the major back to the city, back to the same neighborhood where the British were searching for him. He had the address, and enough gas. Seeing him off, Gideon gave him a pistol, in case anything happened. After his talk with Asher, Brand understood it wasn't for Chadwick. It was for him.

# – 9 –

The next night, while he was safely home in bed, dreaming of Eva at the Edison watching a film of him and Asher's blonde, the two of them strolling the beach where his family used to holiday, smiling at some private joke, Major H. P. Chadwick worried loose the ropes binding his wrists, broke a window and escaped barefoot over the roofs of the Bukharan Quarter. By the time the police arrived, the place was empty, but that didn't matter. The Mandate celebrated their new hero while the *Post* ridiculed the hapless kidnappers. Though it was no fault of his own, and the officers from Tel Aviv were still being held elsewhere, Brand expected the failure would reflect on everyone involved. Following Asher's orders, he hadn't told Eva. Now he couldn't.

Monday he dropped her off at the King David and ate his lunch sitting in the drive, keeping an eye out for Edouard and the blonde. How much did he know, Asher had asked, as if *he* didn't know, or didn't trust Eva.

Brand thought she was stronger than all of them. As close as they'd become the last six months, not once, drunk or sober, had she said a word about her husband. He was her secret as surely as Katya was his, her memory recalled in solitude, tended reverently, like a well-kept grave. It was all he had, sometimes all he wanted—to be with her. Without her the world was meaningless, a round of tasteless meals and restless sleep. Eva was just a substitute. She knew it as surely as Brand did, their love a brittle consolation. Together they tried to remember what life was like, and then when they succeeded, felt guilty. He still thought they should go away, except he'd done that already. Even at sea Katya had followed him, like the stars, invisible by daylight, at night everywhere. If he left now, would he feel the same about Eva?

She came out a good twenty minutes early, by herself, surprising him. Normally she brightened, finding him waiting there. Today her face was set, lips pinched, one arm trapping her purse against her ribs as she stalked to the car.

Before she said a word, she fumbled with a pack of matches and lit a cigarette. She exhaled theatrically, scowling at the curling cloud. Why do people think they can treat me like a servant?"

"Who treats you like a servant?" Her client, he hoped.

"Everyone, everywhere I go."

"I'm sorry." He pulled around a dove-gray Bentley and rolled down the drive.

"They think because they pay you they can treat you any way they like."

Brand thought it was also true of being a cabbie but held off.

"He said he had to do something important, so would I mind seeing myself out."

" 'Important.' "

"I'd like to see his face when he realizes it was me."

She said it with such relish that he wondered if she had feelings for the man.

She sat back, her chin tipped to one side, biting her thumbnail and glaring at the passing storefronts. It was only when she finished her cigarette and stabbed it out in the ashtray that she remembered the pendant. He watched in the mirror as she sat up and fastened it, then slid the chain between her fingers till the clasp was in back.

"You never treat me that way," she said.

"You'd kill me in my sleep."

"I would not. I'd wake you up first."

After his meeting with Asher, he was even more keenly aware of everything he didn't know. He couldn't quiz her on their mission at the King David, and remained alert for clues. Blackmail or reconnaissance, they were making a sustained effort. From what she'd let slip, he expected the payoff would be worth the sacrifice. He hoped so, and soon. He'd come to hate Mondays.

As always, she wanted him to stay, as if, having sold part of herself, she was lonely. He parked and followed her up the stairs, thinking he'd have one cognac. Her flat was hot, and she hadn't eaten lunch. They lay down on her couch, dozing, the sun etching bright panes on the sheer curtains, no sound but the trilling sparrows, and for a moment, holding her, picturing the girl she'd been running through the harvest orchards, he wanted to save her. Was that love? Later he would beg Katya's forgiveness for entertaining the idea, but for an instant he was convinced, despite all the sorrows of the world, that they could be happy.

At five thirty the sirens blew curfew. By six, anyone left on the streets was subject to arrest, though in practice the police detained only Jews. In protest the students jammed Zion Square, tearing up their papers, the khamsin spawning whirlwinds of confetti. The British rolled up buses, and when those were full, stake trucks with wire cages. It was a show. They could detain only so many. Next week they'd release them and do it again.

For the students, being arrested was a piece of theater. They all knew what to say.

"Name," the booking officer asked.

"A rightful citizen of Eretz Israel."

"Address."

"City of David, Land of Avraham."

183

All week Brand tried to stay away from both the new and old cities, but there were checkpoints everywhere. Thursday afternoon, while he ducked through the suburbs, the Irgun released two of the Tel Aviv hostages, dropping off a pair of coffins in the middle of Trumpeldor Street. The hinged lids opened and the officers emerged like the risen dead, wobbly from sedatives, pound notes stuffed in their shirt pockets to cover wear and tear on their uniforms. The radio made it clear. The other three would die if the British refused to commute their sentences.

In the Alaska, the rumor was that a crackdown was coming. Two of the waiters had left for Morocco, a euphemism for disappearing into the kibbutzim. As Brand ate his *Jaegerschnitzel*, he noted several booths usually reserved for regulars were empty.

"Slow night," he said, paying his bill.

"Rabbits," Willi said. "They hear a noise, they go running."

"Not you."

"Where am I going to go? I'm here."

Friday night, when Mrs. Ohanesian's phone rang and she called him downstairs, Brand remembered Willi's philosophy.

"This is Mr. Grossman," Fein said. "There's been a change of plans. I have to cancel my pickup for tomorrow morning."

There was no pickup for tomorrow morning. "I'm sorry. I hope everything's all right."

"Thank you, no. At the last minute some unexpected guests have decided they want to drop by, so tomorrow's no good."

"Would you like it for another day?"

"No, I just thought I should let you know. Now I need to go tidy up. They're supposed to be here early, and everything needs to be put away."

"I understand," Brand said. "Good luck."

His first urge was to run, grab Eva and head for Jaffa, only she was like Willi. Even if Brand managed to get through the checkpoints, she'd never go. He needed some of her stubbornness, some of her outrage. Like so many of his pricklier traits, he'd lost them in the camps, had become a model prisoner, waiting for his bowl of thin soup, waiting for the day to end. The same patience that saved him made him no better than a penned animal. Rabbits, Willi said, and he was right. If Brand had a rabbit hole, he'd vanish down it, like those waiters taking off for Morocco, leaving the police an empty room. They were coming for him, Fein had warned, except he wasn't telling Brand to run. He was telling him to get ready.

He wondered if Eva knew. She had to, yet he was tempted to call Mrs. Sokolov, and then when he did, Eva wasn't there.

"Who shall I say called?"

Mr. Grossman, he was going to say, when there was no reason. "Jossi."

"Oh, hello, Jossi. She's doing some last-minute shopping. You know we're having company tomorrow."

"I heard. Do you have anything special planned?"

"No, we'll just be here and see how things go. I think that's the best plan."

It wasn't the answer he wanted. He saw Asher's face, soft as a rotten apple, and thought of Koppelman.

"Good luck," he said.

"Good luck to you too, Jossi. I'll tell her you called."

He didn't need to dig through his things. He'd been careful all along, from habit, as if his flat being searched were inevitable. He didn't trust his cigar box to the crypt. He wrapped Eva's note and half of the money in oilcloth, tiptoed downstairs and, by moonlight, stopping every few turns of the shovel to make sure it was just the cuckoo, buried the bundle under a mound of dead flowers behind the caretaker's shed.

In the driveway the Peugeot shone. When he turned the key, he pictured Mrs. Ohanesian cocking her head toward the noise like her budgie. There were spots in front of the other boardinghouses, but he didn't want the police to see the car at all, and to be safe moved it to a quiet side street below David's Tomb, checking all four doors before climbing back up the hill.

Still he wanted to run, even if there was nowhere to go. After eluding them for so long, surrendering seemed a mistake. He'd never been tortured, or never professionally, only Nosey kicking at him as they fell out for roll call, forcing him to lie facedown in the snow, a daily, pointless torment. He wasn't like Asher or Koppelman, he was like Lipschitz. He might tell them every-thing, betraying Eva. He didn't know where any of the rest lived. He suspected Asher had set it up that way, his careful plans ruined by Brand falling for her.

In the morning he woke with the sun. Before he could wash, the radio told him the British had shut down the main phone exchanges and begun rounding up suspects. They'd had to fight their way into Kibbutz Yagur. There were reports of casualties.

Fein had been right about the operation but wrong about the scale. Tel Aviv was under a total curfew, an extra affront on the Sabbath. Here they'd cordoned the western neighbor-hoods and raided the headquarters of the Jewish Agency, whose leadership was under arrest. It was a baffling shift in tactics. Instead of going after the Irgun and the Stern Gang, they were targeting the Haganah, a strategy Brand thought

187

idiotic. They might as well try to arrest the whole country. Strangely, the idea gave him hope, as if he were no longer alone.

He dressed, expecting the doorbell to ring at any second. His bed was made, the dishes put away, everything in its place, like a cell ready for inspection. It was the end of the month, so he left an envelope with his rent propped against the radio. He watered the cactus, and though there was no chance of rain, lowered the window so it was open just an inch, then sat down at his table and waited. After a while he got up and lit his Primus stove to make coffee. He was sipping it, looking out over the stony slopes of the cemetery at the Zion Gate, when from the front of the house came the low grumble of a diesel and the squeal of brakes.

How long he'd imagined this. That first time, in Riga, they'd grabbed him on the street. A car pulled up, and he hadn't had time to run. Now he was surprised at how calm he was, how resigned. The jump from his window was no more than fifteen feet. He could hide out in the crypt, a gun in each fist like a Wild West desperado.

Downstairs there was a rapping at the door. He could hear Mrs. Ohanesian saying something, and the burr of a man's voice. Rather than wait for them, he gathered himself and crossed the room. One hand on the knob, he gave the flat a last look, as if he'd never be back, then opened the door.

"Stop where you are," a policeman at the foot of the stairs called, pointing.

Brand raised his hands.

Mrs. Ohanesian touched her heart as if stricken. "What is going on here?"

"This man is under arrest."

"What has he done?"

"It's all right," Brand said, suddenly proud of her. She was more upset than he was.

The policeman was accompanied by an Airborne soldier in a bright red beret. Poppies, they were called, notorious for their bar brawls and overzealous searches. The staircase was narrow, and the two advanced on Brand warily, as if he might resist. He held out his wrists to be handcuffed, but the policeman just took his arm.

The policeman went through Brand's pockets, glancing at his papers, confiscating them.

"I left the rent on the table," Brand told Mrs. Ohanesian as they hauled him off.

"Be quiet," the Poppy said, bending back Brand's hand so it felt like his fingers might snap, making him gasp.

"You're hurting him!" she protested, and followed them out onto the porch.

Brand struggled in their grasp, and the Poppy twisted his hand again, buckling his knees. Brand swore.

"I told you to shut up."

"Stop it!" Mrs. Ohanesian screamed.

In the street a convoy idled, a jeep and a police van escorting a sand-colored bus with wire mesh windows from which a dozen prisoners watched. Brand recalled the old Arab with his box of scarves, the beseeching look he'd given him. Brand didn't want anyone's pity. He wanted to jerk his arm free and shatter the soldier's nose, and would have if they weren't holding him. He planted his heels as they dragged him toward the open door, leaned back, deadweight, knowing he was only making it worse for himself. The prisoners clamored behind the wire, showering down curses. "Nazi bastards!"

The Poppy clamped a hand around Brand's ear and twisted. The pain made everything else secondary. It took all of Brand's strength not to faint. Before he could recover, they shoved him onto the bus and the doors folded closed. As he lay across the stairwell, covered in dust, his ear throbbing hotly, the prisoners gave him a round of applause he saw as mocking.

A man with a freshly split lip reached down from his seat to help him up. "Shabbat Shalom."

Peaceful Sabbath. A comedian.

"Shabbat Shalom," Brand said, brushing himself off.

As they pulled out, a squad of Poppies was crossing the yard for the porch, and while they wouldn't find anything, he wanted to apologize to Mrs. Ohanesian. He hadn't meant to make a scene.

The bus was less than half full, and smelled of burnt motor oil and sweat. He expected to see Fein or Yellin among his fellow passengers, but they were strangers—all of them men, several in rabbinical black, wearing prayer shawls and *kippot*. Some were white-haired, some just boys. All together, they resembled a modest minyan or a Torah class more than a secret army.

At the station road the convoy turned for Montefiore. Normally the sidewalks would be teeming with families in their Sabbath best on their way to shul. Instead, the neighborhood looked evacuated. Just past the windmill, outside a terra-cotta-roofed apartment block, they lurched to a stop. In silence, the prisoners watched the policeman and the Poppy approach the front door and knock.

"Five mils he's a fighter," his bloodied seat-mate offered the bus at large.

"I've got five."

"Make it ten."

He'd forgotten what boredom could do. In the camps they bet on everything from the weather to the rats, all the way up to life and death. He'd thought it wretched, except it helped pass the time.

The man who finally emerged was the size of a

bear, a young Hasid with dark sidelocks and a bushy beard. He dwarfed the Poppy, yet removed his hat and plodded down the walk between them, hanging his head as if guilty.

"Pff," one of the bettors let out.

Another clucked his tongue, and Brand realized their cheers for him had been in earnest.

He'd been willing to go peacefully. Now his anger lingered, growing with each stop. He cheered the ones who fought, joining his voice to the chorus of scorn raining down on the Poppies, as did, later, the big Hasid. No matter how meekly they'd come, behind the wire windows they were a mob, with a mob's cruel sense of humor. They jeered and threw coins when the Poppies' backs were turned, until a squad boarded the bus and went row by row, making them empty their pockets, roughing them up when they stalled. Brand, used to the torpor of the camps, admired their defiance. When it was his turn, he acted as if he didn't understand, answering in Latvian, earning him a cuff on his sore ear which brought tears to his eyes.

At the police station he expected more of the same, but instead of a team of interrogators beating him in a dingy cell, a clerk with bad teeth and perfect posture typed up the information on his papers and returned them to him. Another busload arrived. There weren't enough benches for everyone, and after submitting to finger-printing, Brand had to process outside to a shadeless courtyard and wait in line to get on a different bus. The Poppies stood guard with tommy guns. He thought of Katya and the train station in Rumbula and clenched his jaw. He hoped Eva was safe.

The rumor was that they were going to the detention camp in Rafah, down by the Egyptian border, or the old prison at Acre, above Haifa, on the water and much nicer, according to a fat Yemeni with a gold earring like a pirate. Sarafand, Netanya, Petah Tikva. Again, they bet, as if unconcerned for their own fate. The British had a secret camp in Eritrea reserved for Very Important Jews, but, by grudging consensus, unless their disguises were brilliant, no one on the bus looked very important. It was only when they headed west across the desert that they understood their destination was Latrun, the news triggering relieved laughter. Of all the camps, it was the closest. Brand didn't see it as a victory.

From a distance the camp might have been a kibbutz, a water tower presiding over a dusty arrangement of war-surplus tents ringed by concertina wire. As the bus slowed and two guards walked the gates open to admit them, he felt his throat closing and gulped a lungful of air. On the parade ground, under the baking sun, clerks were waiting for them at tables, ledgers at the ready. As if reliving a dream, Brand knew exactly what would happen next. They'd be separated, their clothes and shoes taken away, leaving them naked as animals, defenseless. Then the selection would begin.

Occupation?

Mechanic, Brand had said, and was saved.

How many others were thinking the same thing? As the bus cleared the gates, a detail of Poppies fell in alongside them, machine guns slung high across their chests. No one heckled them.

Unlike the Germans, the British were surprisingly disorganized. For a long time, though no one complained, Brand's line didn't move. When he finally reached the table, the clerk informed him, apologizing like a waiter, that there were no more uniforms. The tent he was assigned to didn't have enough cots. He and two other men ended up sleeping on the floor with only a thin blanket for a pad, and in the morning his hip hurt.

Latrun was designed to be a resupply base, not a prison. Water was rationed, the latrines overflowing, and still the buses came. The tent reeked of BO, though after a while Brand couldn't smell himself. It reminded him of the transit camp near Trieste where he'd spent a week before shipping out, everyone sick with dysentery. Here the days lay empty before them like the desert, stretching to the horizon on all sides. There were no work details, no books, no playing cards, as if the heat and sheer boredom would make them confess. There was no news, only rumors, and he missed his radio. As he waited his turn to be questioned, he recalled details he needed to forget, like the initials on Asher's valise, and Emilie de Rothschild's being on the train, and Gideon's scar. He knew the Irgun had taken Major Chadwick to Nablus and were planning something big at the King David. He could barely withstand the Poppy wringing his ear. What chance did he have against a trained interrogator?

In the morning, after the tent stood for head count, the master sergeant read off the names of the unlucky few. They said goodbye, settling up any last bets as they stripped their cots and gathered their belongings. Guilty or innocent, they weren't coming back. Every morning Brand expected the master sergeant to call his name, but as the days passed he began to entertain the absurd notion that they'd forgotten him, or were simply too busy. And then, one morning, the master sergeant looked up from his clipboard and called: "Jorgenen."

By his tone Brand was certain he knew the name was a fake. Clever. They'd let him think he was safe to make breaking him easier.

"Here," he said.

"Step forward."

Like a volunteer, he did.

Instead of a dungeon with sweating walls, they took him to a tent on the far side of the parade ground, where, after standing outside in the wilting sun for several hours, he entered the stifling darkness and sat across from a CID officer with thinning ginger hair, an epidemic of freckles and a toothbrush mustache. The man's right hand was bandaged, making it hard for him to turn the pages of the report in front of him, and he smelled of flowery cologne. Brand expected a more sinister inquisitor, and considered that it might be a trick.

"Name," the man asked.

Brand gave it.

"Is this your current address?"

"Yes."

"How long have you lived there?"

"Eight months."

"Have you ever been arrested before?"

"No."

Everything the man asked him was in the report, and yet with each answer Brand felt he was further incriminating himself. The man didn't write anything down, at times didn't even seem to be listening, just watched Brand as he answered, cocking his head, examining the planes of his face like a surgeon.

"You're certain you've never been arrested before."

"Yes, sir."

"May I see your papers?"

Brand unfolded them.

The man glanced from the grainy photo of Brand to his face as if they might be different, then opened a fat binder filled with mugshots. He licked a fingertip and, haltingly, with an insulting deliberateness, leafed through the cellophane-covered pages, sucking his teeth so his mustache twitched, pausing every so often and squinting up at Brand to compare him with the wanted. Finally he closed the binder and set it aside. He held out Brand's papers, then, when Brand went to take them, didn't let go. He drew closer, craning over the table so their faces were inches apart, as if to tell him a secret.

"Jossi Jorgenen," the man said, looking into his eyes like a mindreader, and Brand was afraid to blink.

"Yes."

"Do you know why you're being detained?"

"No."

"You're being detained because someone gave us your name. Do you know who that person is?"

Lipschitz. Asher. But that was exactly what the man was fishing for.

"No."

"Don't you want to know?"

Eva had said they had people inside the CID.

"No," Brand said.

The man let go of his papers and sat back, arms folded over his chest as if he'd won. "I want you to think about that person when they take your picture. I want to see it in your face." With a finger he beckoned a guard. "Goodbye, Mr. Jossi Jorgenen, and good luck."

In the next tent Brand stood still, trying not to think of anything while a photographer blinded him, then followed the guard to the camp laundry to turn in his blanket. He had no personal property to claim, just signed where the clerk indicated and was officially released. The interrogator had scared him, and he was relieved he wasn't going to prison. His fellow parolees waiting for the bus were mostly students. They treated the whole thing like a joke, mouthing off to the guards, singing protest songs. Someone broke into "Hatikvah," and Brand joined in, bellowing it out to show the Poppies they could never take away the people's hope. It was only on the ride back to Jerusalem that the giddiness of being free again wore off, and he realized that, while he hadn't said anything, they had a record of him now.

He walked to Eva's from police headquarters, taking a winding route through the Old City, sneaking down alleys and across courtyards to make sure he wasn't followed. Curfew was over. While he'd been detained, the British had commuted the death sentences. The next day the Irgun released the officers, as if the two sides were even. Brand had been a pawn all along.

Eva was safe. They never searched her place. "You stink," she said, pushing him away before rewarding him with a stingy kiss.

"What about everyone else?" he asked.

She fixed him with a look, as if he should have known. "You're the only one who got picked up."

"Funny," he said, though later, walking home in the lowering dusk, the swallows cutting the air, he wondered what it meant. That he was expendable. That he was a decoy. But why draw attention to themselves at all, unless someone wanted him out? It was possible Lipschitz had given him up, except in that case they would have asked him about Asher. Pincus, Scheib, Greta. Victor, Gideon. Edouard. No matter how Brand turned it over, he couldn't make sense of it, and decided, with the impatience of someone who hasn't slept in days, that it was something the interrogator told everyone.

The Peugeot was where he'd left it, shining beneath a streetlight. Brand felt a surge of pride, as if he'd outsmarted the entire British army. He only glanced at it in passing, as if it wasn't his, promising he'd find time to wax it tomorrow.

Though the porch of the boardinghouse was dark, Mrs. Ohanesian's windows glowed. She caught him before he could reach the stairs.

"Some men came by the other day. They said they were from the police. I told them you were at work." She seemed to want credit for this, as if it were a brilliant gambit.

"What did they want?"

"They asked to see your room. I gave them the key. I'm sorry. I didn't have a choice."

"Thank you for letting me know."

"Of course," she said, with neighborly sympathy. "I'm afraid they made a mess. I cleaned up the best I could."

He thanked her again and climbed the stairs, braced for the worst, and then, when he'd lit the stove and adjusted the wick, he saw the radio. The plastic grille was cracked in half, one corner of its red-and-cream Bakelite casing gone. They'd probably dropped it, an unfortunate accident. Through the jagged hole he could see the tubes inside—still intact, as far as he could tell. Mrs. Ohanesian had kept the broken pieces as if Brand might glue them back together. He didn't expect the radio to work, but plugged it in anyway, turning it on hopefully.

It was dead.

"Bastards."

The rest of the flat was neat. He owned so little that he could tell instantly if something was missing, and as he cast about he noticed the windowsill was bare, the floor beneath swept clean, no telltale dirt. He thought he'd find the cactus in the trash, the pot smashed to shards, but there was nothing. He checked everywhere, discovering, as he went, that his cigar box was empty.

"Rotten bastards."

What would they want with a plant? He wondered if Mrs. Ohanesian had come across it withered on the floor and thrown it out.

"I didn't see anything like that," she said, baffled.

"Did you close the window?"

Of course she had, so it had been open when they searched the place. Now everything made sense. He circled around the back of the house with an electric torch, tramping through the crypts until he was directly under his window, then paced forward, step by step, sweeping the beam over the weeds and rocks and broken glass. The night was dark and he was exhausted, and when the torch dimmed he heeded the sign and climbed the stairs to bed. In the morning he went down to look again, but he never found it.

# – 10 –

She was busy Friday night, so he worked late, trying to make back what they'd taken. Once the sun set, the western suburbs were ghost towns, but the new city was alive with neon, the students packing the jazz clubs ringing Zion Square, smoking on the sidewalks, whipping around him on their motorbikes. It might have been Rome. The reckless excitement of wartime. Each night could be their last. After weeks of curfew, everyone not preparing for the Sabbath was out, and Brand the godless profiteer cashed in, shuttling the swells from the tourist hotels to Ben Yehuda Street restaurants offering black market scotch and caviar straight from the Volga.

In the lull, fashionable Jerusalem's social calendar resumed with a dinner-dance at the King David hosted by Katy Antonius, a widowed Arab socialite who spent her husband's fortune currying the Mandate's favor. Her guest list was catholic and international, a mix of dowagers and diplomats, financiers and journalists whose opinions she courted with chateaubriand and old port. Brand had just let off the Swiss consul and his mistress and was counting his mingy tip, when, three cars behind him, floating up the drive, solemn as a hearse the color of smoke, came the Daimler.

All four doors opened before the valets could reach them, and out stepped Emilie de Rothschild, whom Brand was forbidden to see. She was taller and blonder than he recalled, with the flawless skin of a movie star. She wore black, her skirt slit high up the thigh, exposing a coltish flank. He folded his money and shoved the wad in his pocket, then, knowing he should resist, glanced at the mirror again. He didn't recognize the driver, also tall and fair, possibly American, with a strong chin, but identified the wiry man climbing out of the backseat, dark as a Yemeni in a beautiful pinstripe suit—even before he saw the scar—as Gideon. The last of the foursome, half obscured by the car as she joined the others on the curb, fetching in a red dress Brand had zipped her into a dozen times, was Eva.

A brazen assassination or more reconnaissance, the mission smacked of Asher. The only reason he wasn't there himself, Brand realized, was his face. Like Begin, he had to fight by proxy now. Brand thought it would be harder waiting back in Nablus, though, knowing Asher, he was probably already plotting the next operation.

Gideon took Eva's hand, the driver took Emilie de Rothschild's, and they joined the other couples inside.

Had they seen him, alert, like spies, for every detail, or were they too busy playacting? He could have driven them. Maybe they no longer trusted him, after having been detained, and she couldn't tell him. As he mulled what it all meant, a valet swung the Daimler past him and left onto Julian's Way, signaling and turning up the drive again, giving the car privilege of place at the front of the queue, as if for a quick getaway. It was possible he was theirs too, the plan elaborate, split-second. Since Brand wasn't part of it, he decided it would be better if he cleared out, yet as he rolled the Peugeot down the drive, he was frowning, his brow furrowed as if he weren't sure.

She'd said nothing to him, just as, for her own safety, he'd said nothing about Major Chadwick. He'd felt guilty, keeping that lethal secret from her, though finally Asher was right: she didn't need to know. He couldn't blame her. They all followed protocol for a reason.

For the same reason, the next night, lying beside her, he didn't ask what the mission was, or how late she came home, or with whom. It wasn't just protocol. Since he'd been released she spoiled him, baking cookies and serenading him in bed as if he'd been away for years. She told stories about her brother and her grandmother with the sight and hummed lullabies from her childhood, her head resting on his chest, her hair smelling of vanilla. Drowsy with brandy, he held her in the warm dark, not wanting to break the spell.

Normally she preferred being left to herself Sunday night, but this time she asked him to stay. She made an elaborate coq au vin, and after dinner opened a vintage bottle of cognac she'd been saving.

"What's the occasion?"

"This is what I do every Sunday. You're just never here."

Later, as they slow-danced to the phonograph, her head nestled against his shoulder, she cleared her throat and began hitching, and he realized she was crying. The husband. An anniversary, maybe. He knew to let it pass instead of asking what was wrong, kept swaying and rubbing her back. Before the song ended, she recovered, dabbing at a tear with a knuckle and smiling at her own silliness, her scar forming a twisted dimple. As always, he saw them as if he were hovering in a corner of the room, and wondered what Katya would think. Brand the pushover, Brand the dupe.

"Remember you said we could go anywhere in the world," she said, sniffling. "Where should we go?"

"Right here," Brand said.

"No, somewhere far away. Somewhere no one would bother us."

"Tahiti."

"That's where I want to go."

"We'll go," he said. "I have money."

"You don't have that much money."

"We'll have a grass hut right on the beach and I'll catch fish for our dinner."

"We'll sleep in a hammock," she said.

"And shake coconuts out of the trees."

"You'd get sunburnt."

"So would you."

"I'd turn brown and wear a flower in my hair."

She seemed better, though he knew she was only playing along for his sake. Her tears were real, her laughter an act, while Brand's optimism was false, never quite masking the open grave of the past. When weren't they pretending?

In bed he couldn't get the husband and Katya out of his mind, and then fell victim to a confused nightmare in which Asher's face merged with his, the bruised flesh rotted and soft as an old pumpkin. He was in his car, waiting at the Zion Gate checkpoint. Somehow he knew they knew who he was, and to disguise himself, with his fingernails he began peeling off wet strips of skin. As blood filled his mouth, salty as seawater, Asher's and then his own face disappeared, and the eyes watching him from the rearview mirror were no longer his but Koppelman's, rolling back like they had when Nosey crushed his skull. The Tommies were coming with their dogs. The cars in front and behind were too close, and there was nowhere to go. In the morning he blamed it on the coq au vin and didn't tell Eva.

Like every Monday, they left for the King David at eleven thirty. She liked to be early, so did he, another way in which they were sympathetic. The Zion Gate was slow, giving him a chance to buy a *Post* from an enterprising newsboy, but there was no problem getting through. They took Abraham Lincoln, leaving the Old City behind. It was hot, and they rode with the windows open, her hair blowing across her face like a second veil. He almost wished he hadn't stayed the night. After being so close, it was harder to let go. He would never get used to delivering her. He rolled up the drive and took the last shady spot under the portico. It was almost time.

"Don't look at me like that," she said, fixing her hair in the mirror.

"Why not?"

She shook her pendant at him like a talisman. "Because I love you, stupid."

He laughed as if it were a joke. Inwardly he was thrilled. She'd never said it before.

"Kiss me," she said.

"Here?"

He twisted in his seat so she could reach him.

She held his face in her hands. "I don't want to do this, but it has to be done. Please understand."

"I do," he said, because she was serious. She'd had a double cognac before they left, and this last week she'd been emotional, talking about how she looked for her brother after the war. Brand reciprocated, saying he never found any of his family, but left out the story of Crow Forest. Now he felt selfish.

"Remember Tahiti." She fished in her purse for a compact and fixed her lipstick. "Go eat your lunch. I hate thinking of you waiting for me."

"I don't mind."

"I do. Go, please."

"We'll go out tonight," he offered as she was walking away.

He wasn't sure she heard. She turned and blew him a kiss, waved for him to take off. The doorman opened the door for her, and she was gone.

As if to prove his devotion, he stayed. Stoic Brand. Much as he despised Mondays, he had his routine, and this time of day finding a shady spot was a bonus. The lunch rush was beginning, the lobby bar filling with businessmen. He opened the *Post*, resting it against the steering wheel, and settled in. The high commissioner had flown back to Whitehall for a meeting with Churchill. The Anglo-American committee was visiting Poland to decide the future of European Jewry. As he pored over the stories, last night's dream intruded, his nails digging into Asher's face, peeling away the skin like rind. He was surprised Lipschitz hadn't made an appearance, having haunted him so constantly, or Katya. He never dreamed of his mother and father, only pictured them being marched down the snowy road hand in hand, which was wishful and probably wrong, and had to shake his head, like now, to banish the idea.

He turned on the radio—piano music. Not the soothing movements Mrs. Ohanesian favored, but a wild flurry of notes racing up and down the scale like stairs, and he lowered the volume.

He was in the middle of an editorial speculating on how the Jewish Agency would function with most of its leaders in prison when a Poppy with a tommy gun exited the front doors, stalked to the far edge of the drive and peered over the wall. There was a sunken service entrance below where trucks made deliveries, a fact Brand had noted on his map, and as he imagined the possibilities, the Poppy raised the stock to his shoulder and fired.

The doorman didn't budge, as if this was normal. Brand's instinct was to drop the paper and throw the car in reverse, but, afraid of calling attention to himself, stayed put.

The Poppy let off a second burst. There was a crackling as someone below opened up, making him duck, and the *pap! pap!* of a single-shot pistol. A cloud of thick gray smoke rose from below, eclipsing him for a moment before he retreated, carrying his gun in one hand, barrel down, as he ran for the doors. The doorman let him in as if he were a guest and stood aside again.

After a minute the smoke dissipated, leaving an acrid taste. A smoke grenade. Asher had shown him one in the lab. They were expensive and hard to get.

No other soldiers ran out, no plainclothesmen from the hotel. They were probably in the basement, and Brand thought he should take off while he had the chance, except Eva was inside. She'd told him to leave. He hadn't listened, and now it was too late. From the street, shocking as a crack of lightning, came an explosion like the mail car going up. When he turned toward the noise, he saw a bus listing like a freighter rolled by a tidal wave. It tilted precariously, hung balanced for a second on two wheels before capsizing, landing on its side with a crash that sent a tremor through the Peugeot.

This the doorman couldn't ignore, and though Brand knew the blast was probably Asher's work, he joined him, chucking his *Post* and running down the drive to see how he could help. Across Julian's Way the bomb had blown out the shop windows. People were slowly emerging, groggy with shock. Closer, a dusty jeep sat sideways in the middle of the street. A woman in army khaki staggered toward them, clutching her face, blood pouring between her fingers. The doorman took her arm and helped her to the curb while Brand ran on. The soldiers from the guardhouse were already climbing the bus. The air raid siren wound up, filling the sky with its warning, as if there were more on the way.

"Stand clear!" a Poppy ordered, holding out a palm like a traffic cop, and Brand detoured around the other side, where the rusty under-carriage of the bus was leaking diesel fuel and a soldier above him lowered a moaning Arab woman into his arms. She was old, and light as kindling. Her shoulder was broken, and with his every step she cried out. Not knowing where to take her, he made for the curb and the bleeding Englishwoman until a soldier pointed him through the barbed wire beside the guardhouse to a walkway that led directly to the south wing and the suddenly unguarded doors of the Secretariat.

Was that Asher's plan? Brand imagined the woman—everyone on the bus—was smuggling a grenade under her burkha, except her arm was useless and her cries were real, and before Brand reached the guardhouse another squad of Poppies arrived and took her from him, steering him back to the street. The pool of diesel fuel had spread, and the pavement was a welter of footprints. He expected nails and screws strewn everywhere, but there were just a few jagged scraps of tin—the bomb's container, whatever it was. Someone had set a stepladder against the bus, and a brigade of rescuers was handing down the injured. He helped another grandmother who was more worried about her missing shoes than the gash on her forehead. As he bore her toward the guard-house, promising he'd look for them, a twittering of girlish voices drifted down from above. Across the imposing stone face of the south wing, the Mandate's file clerks and stenographers lined the balconies, gawking at the carnage. Higher up, peering down from the roof's edge with a pair of field glasses, stood a jet-haired woman in bright red lipstick. At that distance it was impossible to tell, but for a second, before he registered her white blouse, he thought it might be Eva.

Impossible, unless she was in disguise. He wouldn't put it past her, or Asher. He wasn't meant to be a spy. They would always be a step ahead of him.

He handed his charge over to a soldier. When he glanced up again, the woman was gone.

In the bus there were dozens of sandals, some of them bloody. The soldiers weren't interested in retrieving them, and shooed Brand to the far sidewalk. A line had formed outside a drugstore, waiting for first aid. From what he could piece together, a man dressed as an Arab porter had rolled a cart of melons up the walk with the bomb hidden inside, lit the fuse and pushed it into the street, then run off behind the YMCA. Brand thought it was probably meant for the guardhouse—the bus had gotten in the way. None of them mentioned the shooting by the service entrance, or the smoke grenade, and he wondered if it was supposed to be a diversion. Asher wouldn't be happy. He hadn't spent all that trouble on a bus.

The Y's bell tower pealed the half hour, its cheery carillon strangely out of place. Seconds later, as if to disperse the crowd, the all clear sounded, a single sustained wail rising from all sides, blaring, going on too long, then finally winding down. On the balconies, clumps of stragglers lingered, not ready to return to their desks just yet. In the street the bus lay in its slick of diesel like a torpedoed submarine. Someone had pulled the jeep into the drive of the King David, and as Brand passed, he saw the dash was dotted with blood. It would smell awful baking in the sun like that all day, an observation he shared with the doorman. Within minutes a red-jacketed valet appeared with a bucket of soapy water and a scrub brush and set to work with an industry Brand admired.

In the Peugeot, as he picked up the *Post*, he noticed he'd gotten some blood on his wrist, probably from the second woman. He licked his thumb and rubbed the spot off, wiping it on the paper, leaving a smudge among the headlines.

He watched, rapt, as the rusty color soaked in, branching along the fibers of the newsprint— the blood of an old woman he'd never met. Was this his work?

It was too easy to blame Asher. Eva was right. He wanted the revolution—like the world—to be innocent, when it had never been.

"Out, out," he said, a thin joke he'd save to tell her later, and turned the page. The top of it caught and he had to smack it with the back of his hand to fold it over. A flock of sparrows on the ledge of the portico spooked, shooting off, and as he smoothed the crease between his fingers, the same lightning that had rolled the bus struck right behind him, rocking the car, the shock wave blowing out his windows, dashing his face against the wheel.

It was bent, and he was bleeding, the taste thick and warm in his mouth. The paper was torn. On the hood of the car lay a sparrow. Asher. How had he ever doubted him?

The blast had knocked the doorman to the ground. He was just getting up, rubbing the side of his jaw as if he'd been sucker-punched. The drive was littered with birds and chunks of stone, chips still raining down, pattering in the trees. Somewhere a bobby's whistle shrilled. Brand struggled to open the door and pushed himself out, used the body of the car to stand and spat darkly, just in time to see the face of the south wing swell and tremble, its skin splitting, cracks spewing white puffs of dust like a dam about to burst. The women on the balconies were screaming. Impossibly, the roofline was cocked. He reflexively took a step back.

The bomb had done its job. Groaning, the girders twisted and gave way. The balconies tipped and pitched forward, spilling their occupants, and with a roar the front of the building buckled, slumped, then plunged to the ground, a shuddering avalanche exposing, for a moment, like a dollhouse, the rooms beneath, sending a cloud of dust and smoke dense as a sandstorm billowing over the portico, blotting the sun, engulfing Brand like a hot, gritty wind.

Blindly, arms out like a sleepwalker, he found the curb and blundered across the walk, groping for the door. The doorman had abandoned his post—or no, he'd just ducked inside. He opened it a crack for Brand. As he dove through, a detective with a pistol almost ran him over coming out, followed by two Poppies with tommy guns. Too late, Brand thought.

The lobby was dark and filling with panicked guests. Though he didn't see any damage, the power was out, the elevators dead. He made for the stairwell, aware there might be another bomb, and wondered if she'd known, if that's what last night was all about. *I love you, stupid.*

Everyone else was coming down, and he hugged the wall, shouldering past them, using the banister to haul himself along. He had no idea what room she was in, only that it had a view of the Old City. He hoped it was in the north wing. He'd start at the top and work his way down, checking everything facing the rear. The higher he climbed, the fewer people there were. He raced up the final flights, taking the steps two at a time. When he reached the sixth floor he was gasping. The hall was murky with dust, making him sneeze, and he had to feel his way from door to door.

Most were closed, only a few open, their guests' possessions like clues. A room-service cart with a glass of red wine, a salad and a plate of bread sat untouched by a cracked window. There was no postcard view of the Citadel, only a brown haze like a dirty fishbowl. Farther down, he found a pipe sitting in an ashtray, a pair of leather slippers and a full bottle of gin. He didn't know what he was looking for besides her, and went on, knocking and calling her name.

The north wing was empty. Still hopeful, he worked his way south along the main corridor. As he neared the elevators he noticed a mirror smashed on the carpet. A blade-like shard reflected his face—powdered a ghostly white and streaked with sweat. The clock on the wall had stopped, stuck at 12:37. The dust was settling, making it easier to see. At the far end of the hall, a smoky light shone. As he crept closer, he realized it was the sun.

Ahead, the floor ended, giving on empty space. Like a man on a ledge, he sidled along one wall and braced himself, craning to take in the sheer drop. Lifted by invisible currents, a flock of papers fluttered through the haze. What was left of the south wing gaped as if it had been shelled, the Mandate's clockworks open to the sky like an ocean liner broken on the rocks, desks and filing cabinets and framed pictures strangely in place. Water poured into the void from ruptured pipes, tangles of wires drooping like vines. A floor lamp dangled headfirst by its cord like an anchor. Below, through the smoke, a dozen fires burned in the rubble. Rescuers were already climbing over the pile. He couldn't imagine anyone had survived, and then he heard, attenuated by distance and the wind, the animal cries of the dying, mercifully drowned out, the next minute, by the air raid siren.

Asher had outsmarted them all. Brand thought he should see it as a great victory—Eva would— yet as he retreated to the stairwell, cupping his nose and mouth against the dust, instead of triumph he felt an overwhelming helplessness which only increased when he discovered the door to the roof was locked.

There was no other way up, and rather than

217

waste time trying to bash the lock off with the nozzle of the fire hose, he checked the fifth floor, empty now, with the same stopped clock and dizzying view of the wreckage. A military ambu-lance and a speaker truck had arrived. The police were clearing the street. The blast had flipped the bus onto the sidewalk so it faced the other way. A body was caught on the Y's iron fence, another stuck to the front of the building. Brand shook his head as if they couldn't be real and kept going.

He had company now, soldiers and hotel detectives with passkeys doing a full sweep. He was afraid they'd think he was a looter, until one stopped him by the shoulders and persuaded him to take a drink from his canteen. He'd forgotten his face. They'd mistaken him for a survivor.

Even missing a wing, the King David was too big. It was taking too long, and he was tired. The air tasted of chalk, and every so often he had to stop and bend over to hawk up a dark clot of phlegm. With each floor he became more convinced she'd sneaked out before the bomb went off, slipped past him in the chaos. She'd be waiting for him in the lobby, or at his car, and then, when he skipped the mezzanine, she wasn't either place.

His trunk was dented and covered with a gray film, the backseat full of broken glass. The sparrow, oddly, was gone, as were all the birds. Maybe they were just stunned, he thought, as if logic might explain anything today.

The doorman strode over as if he were pleased to see him. He'd washed his face, but his neck was caked with dust.

"Sir, I'm sorry, you have to move your car."

"I'm looking for someone," Brand said.

"I'm very sorry, sir. It's curfew. You have to park somewhere else."

Brand thought he could use the jeep to bolster his argument, but it was gone. Besides a pristine old Rolls idling by the front doors, the drive was empty. There was no telling, the valets might have spirited away the birds as well.

Brand slammed his door, sending broken glass tinkling. The Peugeot started up as if the bomb had no effect on it. The steering wheel was out of round, the arc beneath his left hand bent, making him pay attention as he curled down the drive, crunching over chunks of stone. The army had sealed off the street with barbed wire, and he had to wait for a Poppy to let him pass before turning onto Abraham Lincoln and jerking the car into an open spot, his front tire scraping the curb.

The soldier who let him out refused to let him back in.

"My wife is in there," Brand said, brandishing his papers like a ticket. He should have never left. He should have checked the mezzanine. He should have searched the roof and the bar and the gardens and not stopped till they'd thrown him out.

"Wait here," the soldier said, and after several more truckloads of Poppies had passed, returned with a female escort who ushered Brand around the drugstore, avoiding the bus, to the side entrance of the Y.

In a gymnasium full of wailing Arabs, the same officious clerks who booked him at the police station took his information. It was possible she was waiting for him back at her place, in which case he was condemning them both. He was tempted to lie about her address, but finally told the truth, though now she was his fiancée. He described her scar and the dress she was wearing and her pendant, and scourged himself for not remembering her shoes. The clerk gave him a card and asked him to have a seat. Right now they were just starting the identification process.

"I'd like to help with the digging out," Brand said.

"I'm sure we have more than enough capable hands," the man said.

"Can I at least see?"

He would have to wait. They were still policing the area. He could wash up, the man offered. There was food available in the canteen downstairs.

Brand didn't want anything to eat, but couldn't sit still, and used it as an excuse. His plan was to go up the stairs and find a window, but there were guards in the hall. Another escort asked if he wanted to use the washroom, as if that was what was wrong with him, and rather than argue with her, he did. In the mirror stood his ghost, his hair and clothes a dusty gray. He bent his head and slopped water over his neck, scrubbing with both hands. The knot on his forehead held the curved imprint of the steering wheel, a red dent. Looking into his eyes, he understood that being there was a waste of time. He thought of leaving and driving straight to Eva's, and decided as a compromise to call Mrs. Sokolov.

It could be arranged, but, as with any function of the Mandate, he had to wait in line. Finally the escort in the hall led him to an office that overlooked a soccer field and discreetly closed the door. On the desk, in the center of the blotter, was a box of tissues. He dialed slowly, composing himself, half hoping no one picked up.

Mrs. Sokolov answered sharply, as if he'd called the wrong number.

"Is Eva there?"

"I thought she was with you."

"She was."

"I'm sorry, Jossi. Where are you?"

He said he'd let her know if he heard anything. She agreed to do the same.

"Long live Eretz Israel," she said.

"Yes," he said, though he was alone.

He went back to the gymnasium, even more crowded now. The identifications had begun, Red Cross nurses guiding huddled families along the edge of the basketball court and through a pair of doors at the far end of the room. As the minutes passed, he kept expecting the clerk to call his name, or his escort to bring him a message telling him she was safe. By now she could be in Nablus with Asher, celebrating their great success. Brand knew he was being irrational, and with a shake of his head cut the thought off.

It wasn't until three thirty that they let the relatives outside. The bodies were gone, leaving smears of blood on the pavement. The bus was still there, the roof pocked as if with shrapnel. They weren't allowed to cross the street. From the sidewalk, behind a rope, they watched the soldiers break up the smoldering rubble with picks and jackhammers. Masked welders burned through beams with hissing torches, and the air smelled of ozone and molten steel. From time to time a whistle blew and the drilling stopped so the rescuers could gather around a hole and listen. If they heard someone, they dropped their shovels and dug with their bare hands, the scrum tossing rocks over their shoulders till they unearthed the person, to be borne away on a stretcher to a waiting ambulance. Brand saw them rescue only two, both men.

The dead they covered with blankets. In their diligence to hide the victims' faces, the feet stuck out. Most were women. Their shoes all looked familiar to Brand, the worn soles and heels and fashionable straps. In Crow Forest the Germans made everyone take theirs off so they couldn't run. This was different, he thought, and though he didn't want to believe it was Eva's choice, he felt tricked. Forsaken Brand. He hated her for saying she loved him.

As the day waned and dusk came on, the army brought in arc lights and a pair of ratcheting steam shovels and a generator that vibrated the air. A heavy tow truck righted the bus and hauled it away. The bell tower tolled the hours, reminding them how long it had been. Some of the families left, receiving news of loved ones, but most stayed, waiting out the night with Brand, the women keening, holding perfumed handkerchiefs to their noses. The heat of the day dissipated, bats flapping in circles high above the site, and as he watched the rescuers clambering over the pile with their miners' headlamps and electric torches, he thought of Katya and the starless darkness of his grandmother's root cellar, and wondered if Eva had been afraid.

For three days he waited, eating his meals at

the canteen as the Royal Engineers dug around the clock with bulldozers and cranes, though by now there were only bodies. He wanted proof— her pendant or a shred of her dress, her purse with her lipstick and her papers. They found no trace of her, and at sundown on Sabbath Eve, as if it were unholy, Brand gave up his vigil.

The Voice of Fighting Zion broadcast a running tally: fifteen Jews and twenty-six British. The Mandate radio said there were also forty-one Arabs, two Armenians and a Greek, not including the missing. The official response was a dance of propaganda. The Jewish Agency condemned the Irgun as terrorists. Begin blamed the British for not heeding their warnings and evacuating the hotel. The British claimed there were none. To Brand it didn't matter. He was done with the war.

The next morning Eva's name was plastered all over the Jaffa Road, along with an Avidor he'd never heard of, and he thought it was a cheat. It should have been him, just as he should have been with Katya in Crow Forest, the two of them inseparable even in death.

That afternoon he visited Eva's flat a last time, borrowing the key from Mrs. Sokolov. He climbed the stairs, the treads squeaking under his feet. Nothing had been touched. There was the cognac bottle on her little table, the phonograph and the records he'd bought for her, in the sink their glasses from that night. He had the urge to clean the place or take something—the cognac, or her pillow, smelling of her perfume. Instead he locked the door behind him and wound his way back through the alleys.

He expected Asher to contact him, to explain. A phone call, a coded note setting up a meeting. All he wanted to do was talk. After waiting several days to make sure he wasn't being followed, he loaded his pistol and drove out the Nablus Road to the safe house. The iron gate was chained, the windows dark, as if no one lived there. It was a kind of cowardice he would never understand, though he was guilty of it himself. How did you kill and still call yourself righteous? How did you live when you let the people you loved die? As desperately as he wanted to forget, he needed even more dearly to remember. Katya and Eva, his mother and father and Giggi, Lipschitz and Koppelman. He owed them a debt, and promised from now on to live as honestly as possible.

He ditched the gun in the desert, flinging the bullets to the wind like stones. Neither soldier nor prisoner, he was free. In his cigar box he had over three hundred pounds. That night while the city slept, he left an envelope for Mrs. Ohanesian and took the road to the coast, parked the car by the docks and shipped out on a freighter bound for Marseilles. His name was Brand, and he could fix anything.

# — Acknowledgments —

The larger conflict that sets in motion and provides the frame for the action of this novel —the law that makes Brand an illegal—is the issue of Jewish immigration to Palestine. On the release of the White Paper of 1939, Zionists worldwide decried the ncw British quotas (75,000 Jews total over the next five years) as too low. As the Nazis' systematic persecution of Jews grew into outright genocide, for many European Jews the impossibility of securing a visa to Palestine became a death sentence, yet the British refused to budge. The circumstances surrounding the British naval blockade of Palestine (as well as the refusal of the United States to accept large numbers of European Jews during the war, or survivors afterward) and the triumphs and tragedies of the Aliyah Bet ships that ran the blockade are well documented in many contemporary and modern novels and histories, including Leon Uris's famous *Exodus* and Tom Segev's excellent *One Palestine, Complete.*

In researching the brief period of combined underground operations involving the Haganah, the Irgun and the Stern Gang against the British Mandate, I'm indebted to dozens of books, including, significantly, Menachem Begin's *The Revolt*, Daniel Spicehandler's *Let My Right Hand Wither*, Zipporah Porath's *Letters from Jerusalem*, J. Bowyer Bell's *Terror Out of Zion*, Larry Collins and Dominique LaPierre's *O Jerusalem!*, Arthur Koestler's *Thieves in the Night*, J. C. Hurewitz's *The Struggle for Palestine*, R. Dare Wilson's *Cordon and Search: With the Sixth Airborne Division in Palestine*, Eric Cline's *Jerusalem Besieged*, Nicholas Bethell's *The Palestine Triangle* and Samuel Katz's *Days of Fire*.

Readers can find a more detailed account of the bombing of the King David Hotel and its immediate human and long-range political consequences in *By Blood & Fire* by Thurston Clarke.

For their rich bodies of work, especially their writing having to do with the Jerusalem of that era, I'd like to thank S. Y. Agnon, Yehuda Amichai, Aharon Appelfeld, Amos Oz and A. B. Yehoshua.

Deepest thanks to my early readers: Tom Bernardo, Paul Cody, Lamar Herrin, Stephen King, Michael Koryta, Dennis Lehane, Trudy O'Nan, Lowry Pei, Mason Radkoff, Susan Straight, Luis and Cindy Urrea, and Sung J. Woo. Special thanks to Diana Scheide for vintage images of Jerusalem, and to Debby Waldman for her help with the last draft stages of the manuscript. And, as always, grateful thanks to David Gernert and Paul Slovak.

# — About the Author —

Stewart O'Nan is the author of fifteen previous novels, including *West of Sunset*; *The Odds*; *Emily, Alone*; *Songs for the Missing*; *Last Night at the Lobster*; *A Prayer for the Dying*; and *Snow Angels*. He was born and raised in Pittsburgh, where he lives with his family.

LARGE PRINT
O'Nan, Stewart, 1961-
City of secrets

JUN    2016